The Auction

The Vampire Authority

Lillith Mykals Kennedy

Published by Lady Raven M. Darkness, 2021.

THE AUCTION

First edition. March 6, 2021.

Copyright © 2021 Lillith Mykals Kennedy.

ISBN: 979-8201057442

Written by Lillith Mykals Kennedy.

The Auction
Lillith Mykals Kennedy

1

Chapter 1

TATINA POV

Yesterday I was taken from my home forcefully by the vampire authority to cover my father's debt. Today I am here being pampered and groomed to be the most beautiful creature I can be for the sick depraved bidders. I have never had my hair dyed and curled. I have never had my nails done. I have never been to a spa. Yet here I am today, getting pampered. Who knows what kind of hell awaits me. I have heard horror stories about the auction. I have heard about the things that happen to the people who end up here. I am afraid.

Here I am with others just waiting to be auctioned out to the highest bidder. It is not fair. I should not have to be here. My father was an idiot. He could not stop gambling. He lost everything playing poker with the vampire authority elite, he should be here not me. Now I have to pay for his crimes. I have to be here to cover his debts. I should be getting married or going to college, but no the vampire authorities plucked me out of my home on my 21st birthday and dragged me here. Here to this hell to be auctioned off to some sicko.

Maybe I will get lucky and end up with a lovely family that needs a nanny or a maid. At least I will have plenty of food and a roof over my head. The worst that could happen is I could be killed. Drew was so excited to get his hands on a hybrid—my mother a fairy and my father a vampire. I am an only child. I have the powers of a fairy and vampire qualities. Unfortunately, I cannot get myself out of this mess. Horace drugged me as soon as I got here to suppress my abilities. No hybrid

3

will stand against the vampire authority. If I did, he would kill me and my family.

"Are you okay?" the young blonde girl painting my nails ask me.

"I guess. I have no choice but to be fine," I reply. I should not be mean to her. It is not her fault I am here. That fault lies with my terrible father.

"True, but you are stunning. I am sure you will be fine," she says. She tries to smile at me and give me hope, but we both know there is no hope for me only doom.

"I am scared," I say. I begin to cry. Why am I crying? I am crying because I am about to be auctioned to the highest bidder.

"Shhh. You do not want Horace coming over here. Please calm yourself. Besides, you do not want to be all puffy when they take your picture," she says. She begins wiping my tears and locks over my shoulder to make sure no one heard me crying. She is right, I do not want any trouble. I only want to get this over with quickly.

I am trying to listen to all of the advice the auction workers are giving us. I need to remain calm and smile. I need to prepare myself for what comes. The first chance I get, I can run. If the drugs would wear off, I could free myself from this place. I can fight my way out. I feel a pinch. I look to my left; he got me again. He will keep me drugged. It doesn't mean whoever gets me will keep me drugged. I can do this. I can survive.

"Now, look at your nails. They are perfect. I will get Lisa to come to do your makeup, and JoJo will do your hair. Okay?" she says. She is way too perky for someone that helps these terrible people.

I nod. I am not in the mood to talk to anyone. Here comes Horace again.

"Smile, girl. You are the big-ticket tonight. You will bring in a lot of money. There are vampires coming from everywhere to bid on your sweet ass," he says. He smells of whiskey and his teeth are gross. When he gets close to me his breath makes me gag.

I give him a fake smile. I wish I had my powers. I would enchant his ass into a fairy trap. I would love to see him suffer. I would love to see them all suffer, but I can do nothing. I am at their mercy.

"Are you scared? Nothing to be scared of unless one of the weirdoes gets you, like me," he says with an evil laugh. I believe him. I would not want to be his little pet.

JoJo comes up behind me and starts pulling at my hair.

"Don't you worry about him? He is not allowed to bid anymore. Not since he killed that girl a few years ago. She was so precious. She was 28 and indebted heavily to the vampire authority. It was sad. Really sad. Horace bought her, and well, nobody ever heard from her again. The vampire authority took him off the auction list, and now he is stuck working here for them forever," she says.

"How did you end up here?" I ask. Maybe I should not ask her why she is here, but I want to know why she is involved. I am curious how this works and why.

JoJo starts twisting my hair up in braids. "I owe but not a lot. So I can work here a few years and be done. The vampire authority gave me the option to go in the short term auction, but since I am a hairdresser, they needed me here instead," she says,

"Oh. My father sold me," I respond looking down into my lap. I cannot believe he sold me.

"I am sorry to hear that. Too bad the authority couldn't take your father instead," she says.

"Yeah. I know. I hate my father for doing this to me. My mother stood by and let it happen. I think she was jealous of me because I am a hybrid. I did not ask to be a hybrid or to be born or to be in this mess," I say.

"None of us asked for this, but here we are. The only thing I can do for you is make you beautiful," she says.

Jojo twists and braids my hair into a Viking hairstyle. I never knew my stringy long dark hair could look so beautiful. She is good at this. I hope she can get out of this life soon.

Lisa comes over to start my makeup. She does not say much. She looks at my skin dabs some stuff on my face. It is so icky. I have never been one to wear a lot of makeup. She has painted my eyes dark and put on red lipstick. I look in the mirror after Lisa finishes. "Done," She says.

"I look like a whore," I say to her.

"That is what you are, a whore, hybrid," Lisa says. She walks away leaving me looking at myself in the mirror. I am a virgin not a whore.

Chapter 2

I STOP IN FRONT OF a mirror. I look like a painted-up hooker. There is nothing beautiful about the way I look. I have on too much makeup and way too revealing clothes. This is ridiculous. I stand in the hall waiting with other people. Men, women, and creatures that I am not sure what they are waiting to have their picture taken for the auction. Every time I pass a mirror, I look at myself. I am disgusted by my appearance. They paint us up like dolls and then buy us to do who knows what to us. Why is this allowed to happen?

"You look sexy, hybrid," Horace says, smiling at me with his nasty teeth. He makes me sick. I hope someone kills you.

I cannot even stand the way he looks at me. He gives me the creeps. No worries, Horace, if I ever get out of this, I will find you and send you far, far away. I will make sure you pay for this someday.

"Can't you even say thank you," he says loudly. I guess he is not used to being ignored by the people of the auctions.

" Hey bitch," Horace yells at me. I keep ignoring him.

"Hey, bitch. I am talking to you. Turn around and say thank you or else," he screams at me and gets right in my face.

A lady comes out of the small room. "Tatina, you are next, honey. Come with me," she says. Thank goodness. I know Horace is ready to kill me. I give Horace a bite-me look and follow her into her office. "You okay?" she asks as she looks back to see Horace mad as hell.

I nod. "Okay, stand on the X, and I am going to make your picture. Smile if you can. I know this is stressful. So do your best," she says. She is sweet and the while selling me to someone, she is sweet to me. Does she even care that she is a part of the process that is dooming me to hell? How can she sleep at night?

I stand on the X and smile while she takes my picture. All I can think about is how can all of these people come in here and work the auctions? How can they live with themselves as they paint us up and sell us?

"There is nothing to worry about here. We screen people very carefully. Do not believe everything you hear. Most of the people who come to us are looking for help. They need a nanny or a maid. It is rarely something sinister. I can almost promise you that you will end up in a good place. You are the top-billed ticket tonight. We do not get hybrids very often anymore. Especially one like you," she says.

"Thank you. That makes me feel better. I am petrified," I say.

"No reason to fret. You are beautiful and young. You are what 21? I hope your auction turns out well," she says.

"I turned 21 yesterday. That is when the authority came to get me," I respond.

"Oh yeah. I remember you are James's daughter. He had so much potential with the authority. Shame he wasted it and now lives in poverty. See, this is a good thing. You can pay off his debt and be happy and far away from him," she says.

"Pay off his debt. Do you mean I am not trapped forever in this? I can leave and have a life," I ask.

"No. Just until you pay off your debt. Honestly, you should fetch enough to take care of it in just a few years. Honey, this is going to be a good thing for you. Just smile. Be kind and obey whoever is lucky enough to get you. You can do this," she says.

This auction might be a blessing. Indeed whoever buys me will be well off enough to treat me right. I am away from that idiot father and my mother. She has followed him around and allowed us to live like pigs for so long. This ordeal might be my saving grace. I need to be polite and perky.

I can do this. "Thank you. I feel so much better. I did not understand, and no one explained anything to me," I tell her.

"Good Now, why don't we retake your picture, and you can smile a big beautiful smile," she says.

I stand on the X again, and this time I smile.

"That is perfect sweet girl. I know that you will land you a big fish," she says.

I laugh. I just want to end up with someone nice. I do not mind cooking and cleaning or tending to kids. I wish to be able to eat and have a roof over my head. I can do whatever it takes to survive. I only want to survive. Please let me survive.

"You can go to the waiting room. When the auction is over, I will come to get you. It won't be long now. I should have everything uploaded for the bidding to start within the hour," she says.

"Thank you for being so kind. Almost everyone had been kind except one person. Thank you so much," I say.

"Don't pay Horace any attention. He is just mad he is stuck here after what he did," she says.

"What did he do?" I ask.

"Trust me. You do not want to know. Just be careful and stay with the group. If he gives you any trouble, Scream loud," she says.

"I will stay with the group," I tell her.

"Good luck. Not that you need it. You got this in the bag, girlie," she says.

I exit the office and walk past all the different people and creatures waiting to have their photographs taken. I wonder how they ended up here. I am sure a lot of them have it worse than me. Everything will be okay. The auction will be over in a few hours, and I will be starting a new life. I can do this.

Chapter 3

I WALK INTO THE WAITING area and look around at all of the people waiting for their auctions to be over. Well, at least there is food. I wish I could put on something more comfortable. This ridiculous costume they put on me is uncomfortable, and it itches. I get it they want to make money off of money, but if someone is looking for a maid, why would she need to look like this. I scan the room, looking for a place to sit and wait. I would love to rest for a while before I leave. I have no idea what is to come, and I think a nap would be the best thing for me.

"Hey, hybrid! Come here," Horace screams at me. I hope he is talking to someone else.

I turn around to make sure he is talking to me. Of course, he is. I am the only hybrid here tonight. I smile politely. "Coming, sir," I say in my sweetest voice.

I walk up to him and smile. He grabs my arm. "Time for your shot," he says. He pulls me into the hall. Oh No, I have to stay with the group. I am terrified as he pulls me down the hall. Tears begin to flow down my face.

"I can wait here while you go get it. She told me to stay with the group. I do not want to get in trouble," I say.

He keeps pulling me harder down the hall. "Come with me, or else I will make you regret your defiance," he yells at me.

I comply. I do not want to make him mad. I have to survive the next few hours, and then I will no longer have to deal with him.

"Those girls painted you up nice. I thought you were a little ugly when you came in but now look at you. You look good enough to eat," he says.

I do not respond. No matter what I say, he will take it the wrong way.

"Hey, I just complimented you. Say thank you, hybrid bitch," he says.

"Thank you. I did not realize you were complimenting me. I apologize, sir," I say.

"Hey, look here. Do not be a smart ass. I am trying to be nice to you. I could be very mean to you. Do you want to see me be mean to you? I bet you like it rough," he says.

He pulls me around the corner and reaches into a cabinet. He pulls out a vial and a syringe. He takes his time getting the shot ready. He is almost drooling, looking over my body. I feel so gross right now as he grabs my arms and stabs me with the syringe.

"There that should keep you under control until the auction is over," he says.

"Thank you," I say.

"You want something to eat. I have food in my office," he says. He is up to something. I already know that. Why else would he pull me away from the group? He is going to hurt me; I know it. Please do not hurt me! Somebody has to come and see what is happening to me.

"No, No, I want to get back. I am supposed to stay with my group. The lady told me to stay with my group. I do not want to get in trouble," I tell him, stuttering and almost begging for my life.

"I am not trying to get you in trouble. I just thought you might give me a taste before you leave," he says. His hand pushes my hair back away from my neck, and he licks his lips.

"A taste? What do you mean a taste?" I ask. I know what he means. He wants to fuck me.

"Do not pretend with me. You have whore written all over you. I bet you are a nasty girl. Aren't you? I bet you are a real nasty little whore," he says.

He grabs my face and tries to kiss me. I push him back, but he presses his lips to mine. I kick him in the shin, and I break free, then start running away. I have to get back to my group. "Please stop. Do not hurt me," I scream as I try to run away, but he is faster than me.

Horace tackles me and climbs on top of me. "Shh, little whore. I am going to get myself a taste of you hybrid. I am going to have some of that special tasty treat you got between your legs," he says.

He starts pulling at me, trying to undress me. "Please stop!" I scream.

Horace manages to get my panties down. He is going to rape me, and there is nothing I can do about it. "You are going to be mine. Either shut up and take it or we can do this the hard way whore," he slaps my face.

I scream, "Help me, Please Help me!"

He is holding my arms above my head as he tries to undo his pants at the same time. "Please stop!" I scream.

I can feel him getting ready to insert his member into me. This is not how I want to lose my virginity. Not like this on a cold floor by some monster. Somebody has to help me. I close my eyes and cry out for help.

"Help ME PLEASE!!" I cry out as loud as I can scream.

I close my eyes and prepare for him to take it. I can feel his hot breath on me and his hardness at my entrance. I cannot believe this is happening to me. Why? What did I do to deserve this?

BOOM

"Get off her, you idiot. I will not miss the next time," she says. I open my eyes as Horace gets off of me. He backs away slowly and pulls up his pants.

"Thank you," I say as I get off the floor and run to her, crying.

"I told you to stay with the group," she says, scolding me.

"I know he did not give me a choice. I am sorry. Thank you," I say again.

"Go back to the waiting area. If anyone stops, you tell them you were with me, Jayne. Your auction is about to start, dear and you need to be close by in case the bidders ask for more pictures. I will deal with Horace," Jayne says.

"Thank you. I am sorry," I say.

"No need to be sorry. Now get back to the waiting area, and do not leave your group again. I might not be around next time one of these assholes tries to rape you," she demands.

"I promise I will stay with the group," I say.

I run back to the waiting area. I try to fix my clothes and wipe my face. I cannot believe what just happened to me. Thank goodness Jayne heard me scream. I do not know what would have happened if she hadn't come to help. I do know what would have happened. He would have had his way with me. He would have raped me. I would have lost my virginity on the cold floor, roughly and unwillingly.

Chapter 4

I GO BACK TO THE WAITING area. I am so thankful Jayne was there to save me. What would have happened if she would not have been there to rescue me. I know what would have happened. That nasty pig was planning to rape me. I have to stay with the group. No matter what, I cannot leave the group.

I wait for what seems like forever. Almost everyone has left the room but me. Some looked happy and others were upset about their destination. I do not know how to feel. I only know that I am all alone in this. I could take a nap while I wait. I move over to a couch and lay down. I can close my eyes just for a second. "Tatina, honey wake up," Jayne says as she nudges me softly.

"Hey, I have some great news for you. Come with me," Jayne says. She looks happy. Maybe I am okay. I try to stay positive as I open my eyes and gather my thoughts.

I was sleeping so sound. I don't think I was even dreaming. I was just in a deep solid sleep. I am exhausted from the day and all the shots that Horace has given to control me has made me sleepy.

"I am coming," I say, still groggy

My brain feels all fuzzy. It must be from the shots wearing off or worry, maybe I am confused. I rub my eyes and try to come alive.

"Tatina Honey, Mr. Craig Madallion has won your auction. He is sending a man up to pick you up. He is very nice. He has a home in New Orleans. We need to get you into something more comfortable. Follow me," she says.

"What do you know about him?" I ask. She seems to know him. Maybe she helped me.

Jayne leads me to her private room, and she hands me a bag. "Change, and I will get you something to take all of that makeup off of your face," she says.

Jayne leaves me to change. I strip off the garb I am wearing and look in the bag she gave me. There is a pair of black leggings, a purple top, a sports bra, cotton panties, socks, and shoes. Thank goodness for something normal to put on. I was almost afraid of what might be in the bag.

Jayne comes back with a warm cloth and makeup remover. "Here, this should do the trick. She put a lot of makeup on you. You are such a pretty girl, you really do not need any of that," she says,

"Thank you. My face was starting to itch from all this stuff on my face. I have never been one to wear a lot of makeup. It just feels icky," I tell her.

"Well, you are far too beautiful to have all of that on your face," she says.

"Why are you so kind to me?" I ask. I wonder if she is being nice because she is nice or because she has an alternative motive.

"Tatina, you deserve some kindness in your life. It would be best if you were not here. What your parents have done to you is horrible. I have to confess. When I found out you were in the auction, I called Craig and encouraged him to bid. He was my brother-in-law. My sister died last year, and he could use a sweet face in his life. I think you would be perfect for him," she says. She touches my face as tears stream from her eyes. She wants to help me.

"I don't understand why you want to help me. I am nobody," I say.

"Listen, Craig has a nice home, and he has plenty of money. He will take good care of you, but Craig is not a cakewalk. He loved my sister. They were very happy. He can be bullheaded, trust me, and it was hell getting him to bid on you. But I am convinced that you two need each other. That is what I told him he needed help and you needed someone to help you. He will help you get educated. He will be a friend. But and there is a big, but in all of this, he can be a real ass," she says.

"So, how do I handle him?" I ask. I am curious if he is such an asshole, how on earth will I be able to handle this lonely man?

"Just be sweet and sassy. Be kind and considerate. Be you and it will all work out," Jayne says.

"Is he a vampire?" I ask.

"Yes, and my sister was a Fairy just like you; we come from very similar backgrounds, you and I. We have the same Fairy clan blood. That is why it is so important to me that you be okay," She says.

"Are you a hybrid?" I ask.

"No, but my sister was a hybrid. I was not born like the two of you, lucky me," Jayne says.

"Oh. I don't understand how it skips some people," I say.

"Me either. My sister was a hybrid, and I am just a Fairy, even though we have the same parents. I only got the Fairy genes. I don't mind. I am not sure I could handle being both. She did it well. Just like you will," She says.

I try to pull my tangled hair back. Forget it. I will handle it when I get where I am going. I am sure he will allow me to shower and wash this mop when I get there.

"They are here for you, Tatina. I hope everything goes well. Just remember to be yourself and be kind. Craig will love you," Jayne says.

"Thank you, Jayne. I hope to see you soon. Just not here," I tell her.

Jayne hugs me and kisses me on the cheek. "You will. I live very close to Craig. When I am home, I will be checking on you to make sure everything is going well," Jayne says.

"Promise?" I ask.

"I am only a phone call away. Craig will get you a cell phone when you get there. We can text each other. I want to know how you are doing," she says.

A man in a black suit comes into the room. He looks like the secret service. "Jayne, I am here for the pickup," he says.

"Tatina, Your ride is here," she says. She kisses me again on the cheek and smiles.

"Thanks for everything," I say as I walk out with the man in the black suit. I am afraid, but I know now that everything will be okay. I can survive this.

Chapter 5

ARRIVING IN NEW ORLEANS to start my new adventure, I have no idea exactly how I should feel. As we drive across the bridge into the city, I feel so many different emotions. The bridge we are crossing is enormous. It is like nothing I have ever seen before. As we travel into the city, I feel this feeling, a new vibe. The feeling that maybe I belong here. I have not been here before, and I am unsure why I feel this way, but I almost feel as if perhaps I am glowing as we drive into New Orleans, my new home.

I knock on the glass separating me and the driver, "Sir, may I ask how much further until we are home?" I ask.

He rolls down the divider. "We are almost there. Traffic might hold us up some, but we should be at the mansion soon. You are going to love New Orleans," he responds.

"Thank you," I reply.

I sit back in my seat as he rolls the glass back up. He has not been very friendly or talked much during the ride, but I have enjoyed the quiet ride. I have not even been that nervous. Honestly, this overwhelming feeling of belonging is putting me at ease. I am just happy to have the auction behind me. Now to move onto the next part.

I can see the massive traffic coming ahead as we drive further into the city. There are a lot of cars. I have lived in the country most of my life, and this is very different. The driver pulls off the main road onto our exit. The homes are multi-colored and beautiful. I cannot wait to walk around and exam the homes closer. I hope to have some freedom.

As we pull into a residential area, I see the most prominent homes I have ever seen in my life. I have never lived in anything big. We lived in a shack. My dad could have easily provided for us, but he made his choice to gamble and lose everything to the vampire authority. This will be my first time in a mansion and I am excited to see what it looks like on the inside, what my room will be like, and how I will live.

The driver pulls into a blacktop driveway. The driveway is long and circles around the back of the house. Three women are waiting for me. The home is enormous. How many stories is this? It has to be more than three. There are balconies and huge windows. I bend my neck to see as much as I can of this magnificent home.

The driver comes around to my door and opens it. He doesn't say anything, just opens the door. A small woman comes up to greet me. "Tatina, welcome," she says.

"Thank you. I am excited to be here," I respond.

"Austin will get your things. I will show you around. You will meet Mr. Craig this afternoon," she says.

"Okay. That sounds great. I am exhausted, to be honest. Can I freshen up? I could really use some water," I say.

"Sure. My name is Lila. I will be your personal assistant while you are here with us," she says.

"Lila, what a beautiful name. Why would I need a personal assistant?" I ask.

"Well, dear, you will be busy and it is up to me to keep you on track at all times. Mr. Craig does not like it when we are tardy or behind schedule," she says.

Lila leads me into the house. We pass two other women she does not introduce me to either of them. The house is like something out of a movie. There is a giant staircase as soon as I enter the home I feel like a princess all of a sudden. Maybe I am a princess and this is my fairytale.

"Tatina, if you will follow me up the stairs, I will show you to your room. You can shower and change. I need to go over the rules of the house with you also. Mr. Craig had clothes delivered for you this morning. One of the maids placed the clothes in the closet for you. You are only to wear the clothes he purchased you. You are free to go out, but you have to be back in the house by dark every night. You are to be in your room every night, and you are to lock the door. Do you understand the rules as I have stated them or did I need to explain each rule to you?" she says, sternly.

This is strange but okay. I understand that I am in a new place, and they are just looking out for me, but why do I have to be in my room with the door locked.Why do I have to be back before dark? Strange does not even begin to cover it, but I do not want to upset Mr. Craig, after all he saved my life.

"I can tell that brain is working behind your eyes. Tatina, we have vampire guests, and you would be a treat to them. We have to keep you safe. You are a virgin, right?" she says.

"Yes, I am, but what does that have to do with anything?" I ask.

"Tatina, when you were being auctioned, vampires wanted to buy your virginity. Do you understand that Mr. Craig wants to protect you and keep you safe? A vampire or a wolf for that matter could do a lot of harm to a hybrid like yourself," she says. There is not a lot of emotion in her words. She is almost stoic. I bet she is a lot of fun.

"I understand and I will obey the rules," I respond.

"Listen to me. We will protect you. You are very valuable. You have no idea. A vampire baby with a hybrid would fetch a big payday for someone. Hybrids are slaves to vampires and treated terribly. You are one of the lucky ones,," she says.

"Wait. Why does he want to protect me? He does not even know me. Why would he care?" I ask.

"My dear, you are from the same clan as his wife, and he wants to protect you. He is a kind man. Just be kind to him. He has had a hard time since she died. You will be his in every way so be prepared to give yourself to him in return for his protection," she says.

At the top of the stairs, we come to a yellow door, "This is your room. You have a private bath. You can use your phone to call down to the kitchen if you get hungry. You have a new cell on the desk. I have already charged it and programmed Jayne's, mine, and Mr. Craig's number in it. You should be all set. Freshen up, and I will come back later. We can see the rest of the house. There is a mini-fridge with water and soda in it," she says.

"Thank you," I say.

Lila leaves, and I go into my new room. I am not sure if I should be thankful or terrified or maybe both. I look at my room. This is my life now.

Chapter 6

LILA POV

I leave the new girl alone in her room. I don't think she realizes what is to become of her and how this will all play out. Stupid bitch!. They never know when they come here that their lives are about to turn into a fiery pit of hell and I am the ruler of her hell. She will be the perfect little breeder. They are all full of hope and joy. Damn, the phone is ringing. I run down the hall to grab it. It is probably Craig. I am sure he wants to check in on his new cash cow.

I pick up the old black phone. I glance around to make sure no one is around. "Hello," I speak softly.

"Lila, Is the new girl settled into her room?" Mr. Craig asks.

"Yes. I have her. She is in her room settling in. She is quite beautiful, Mr. Craig. She will make you and me a lot of money. She is perfect for breeding. I am sure of it. I have not checked but I can smell her ripeness," I say, almost giddy thinking about the money we are about to make off this one.

"Good. I will be back tonight. Make sure she is comfortable. DO NOT scare her. Be nice if you know how to be nice. Check on her often. Make sure she has everything she needs. Got IT!" he says demandingly. He hangs up before I can respond.

He acts as if I do not know my job. I have helped him gather perfect breeding bitches from the auction. Of course, this is the first time Jayne got involved. Poor Jayne. She thought she was sending him a wife and a companion; little does she know what he is really up to and what he wants from her. At least we did not have to pay someone to bid this time. This time an insider brought us the perfect little breeder. Thank you Jayne.

I will keep little Miss Tatina busy and happy. She is in the city with me, of course, she will love it here. I will make sure she is happy. I will be her best friend and then she will agree to anything we want. Craig, he is so sly with the breeders. He can get them to bend to his will. He is sexy and kind; until he gets what he wants them, then it is over. I cannot wait to watch him crush her. It is always fun to watch. They are so happy and thinking they are in for a great life and then boom breeding box for you bitch.

Tatina POV

The room they fixed me is absolutely beautiful. I cannot believe all the clothes he bought me. I have never had this many clothes and shoes before. I grab a pair of blue jeans from the closet and a white top. I go over to the dresser and grab a bra and some cute panties from the drawer. I need a shower and to freshen up a little before Lila comes back to get me to show me the rest of the house.

I walk into the bathroom. Oh my goodness. The bathroom is as big as my room. A beautiful mirror well lit with makeup and hairbrushes. The shower is full of shampoos and body washes. I am going to shower with all of it. Next to the shower is a robe and slippers, just for me. I have never had a beautiful robe or slippers before. There are multiple lotions and body sprays. I must be in heaven. This is unbelievable.

I remove my clothes and turn the shower on, steaming hot. I step into the shower and let the water run down my body. I grab a purple bottle of shampoo and start scrubbing my hair. It smells so wonderful. I rinse my hair and grab a conditioner. The conditioner smells lovely. I let the conditioner soak in my hair. I grab a bottle of raspberry body wash and soak the pink sponge in massive amounts of body wash. I scrub every inch of my body. I rinse the conditioner out of my hair and continue to let the hot water run over my body. I think I could stay in this hot water forever. I never got to shower like this when I was living with my parents. It was never hot water. This is heaven.

I step out of the shower. I dry off with one of the enormous white towels. I grab the pink silk robe and slip into it. I towel off my long hair and sit down in the mirror. I grab a bottle of lotion from the counter. Raspberry. I love the smell of raspberries. I rub my body with the lotion. I smell fabulous.

I towel dry my hair and open the drawers on the counter. I find face cream and apply it. There is makeup here, but I am not a fan of a lot of makeup. Maybe just some mascara. I use some mascara lightly. I finish toweling my hair.

I slip into my clothes. I grab the blow dryer and dry my long hair. I get up from the counter and dress quickly. I have dilly-dallied enough. I need to eat and see the rest of the house.

When I come back into my room, Lila is waiting for me.

"I see you showered," she says. I am not sure if she is being hateful or if it is just her personality.

"Yes. I feel amazing," I say.

"Good, Mr. Craig wants me to take you to dinner. Slip into some comfortable shoes, and we will walk to a restaurant to eat. Is seafood okay?" she says.

"Yes. That would be great," I respond.

I slip into a pair of comfortable shoes. I smile at her. Something seems off with her. Maybe she is just nervous about having me here. I hope she does not think I am trying to take the place of his wife. I did not plan to come here; I just landed here.

"I am ready," I say.

"Good. Let us get going. It is only a mile to Miss Zada's Seafood house," she says.

I follow Lila out of the room and down the stairs. I am ready to see the neighborhood. Maybe I can get to know her and she will be more at ease with me instead of so hateful.

Chapter 7

TATINA POV

Lila walks quickly as we jet down to the seafood bar. I wonder why she is acting so strangely toward me. Did I do something wrong? Maybe she does not want me here at all. I am being paranoid. Probably nothing going on with her, it is just me freaking out over my new life. I have lived my life being around people acting weird. She seems to care about me and everything going on with me. I am probably just, I don't know, being ridiculous. We walk up to a bar at the end of Bourbon Street. This has been the longest walk ever. Maybe it has not. Perhaps I am being dramatic. I am tired and extremely hungry.

We arrive at the seafood bar, and it is all blacked out. The windows are black, and there is no sign. Lila doesn't seem bothered by it. But for me, I find it somewhat disturbing about all of this. It seems off to me. Of course, I have never been here before, so maybe this is perfectly normal. A man walks out of the seafood bar's door and he looks very pale. He scares me.

"Lila, I do not mean to sound ungrateful, but why is well why this place is all well you know ....it is blacked out. And to be honest, it is giving me the creeps. Did you see that creepy pale man? I am afraid. Are you not afraid? Is this normal?" I ask. I am trying to be as respectful as possible.

"It belongs to a vampire, my dear. Do not be alarmed; they all know who you belong to and no one fucks with Craig or anyone who is in his house. Especially you, Tatina, you are his prize procession," she says.

Belong to, what does that mean and his prize procession. I guess I am his procession. He did bid on me in an auction after all. Okay, I guess I do. I think I do belong to him. For now, I belong to someone. It almost feels nice to well belong to someone. I do not feel like a burden in any way at all. I feel like my life is falling into the right place. Maybe all of this will be good for me. I will have to see where this takes me.

"Okay. I was not trying to sound like I did not trust you. Please do not think that, but I have never been much of anymore in my life. I have lived a very sheltered existence, so please pay me no attention if I offend you in any way," I say.

She gives me this smile like I just made her mad or something. I can't figure her out. She is so nice to me but she is off. Something is really off with her. For now, I have to just let it go. There is nothing I can do about this current situation I am in. So I will go with it.

"Tatina, I would never put you in any kind of danger. You have to believe that. Mr. Craig put me in charge of making sure you are safe and I take my job and his orders very seriously," she says.

I do not know. Something is so off. But maybe just maybe I am just on guard. I will trust her for now. Until she gives me a reason not to trust her, but I will be listening and paying attention to every little thing she says and does around me until I figure this out.

"OK. I was just wondering why it was all blacked that is all. Why are we going to a vampire place?" I ask.

"Sweetie, they have the best food. Are you afraid of vampires? You were raised by a vampire and now you are owned by a vampire, I would certainly hope that vampires do not scare you," she replies.

That makes no sense but I smile and agree. Why would vampires be operating a place for humans to come to eat unless they had a motive? And what is her motive for bringing me here? Now I feel like there is a motive and she is not a good person. Maybe all of this is a lie, even Mr. Craig. She is up to something and it is no damn good. I wonder if Mr. Craig is involved. Am I in danger?

I go to the dark restaurant. The worst thing that could happen is a vampire tries to feed on me or kill me. I am not sure if that should be the least of my worry. I should be worried about a vampire trying to breed with me. Surely Lila would not let one of them rape me. I do belong to her boss unless she brought me here to sell me. I feel like I am going to be sick.

We go in and we are seated by a girl that I am sure is not a vampire. At least I do not think she is. She hands me a menu. She does not give Lila one. That is odd. Why didn't she give Lila a menu? This day gets stranger and stranger and Lila is making me more and more nervous.

"Are you eating or did you only come to watch me eat?" I ask Lila with just a hint of sarcasm.

"Yes, but I come here a lot and they already know what I want," she responds.

She glares at me. If looks could kill I would be dead.

"Sorry, I just did not want to be a burden. If you do not want to be here we can get it to go," I say.

Lila tolls her eyes at me.

"Tatina, do me a favor and stop talking. You are starting to piss me off and I promised to be nice to you," Lila says.

"Sorry," I whisper.

Chapter 8

THIS LITTLE GIRL NEEDS just to be grateful we are being so kind to her. A young woman in her position could have ended up in a terrible place. We will get what we want from her, but we will not hurt her. She will be set for life. All she has to do is breed a few hybrids, and she can be on her merry little way. She could have ended up in an underground auction, raped, beaten overbreed, and then tossed in a whore house. She better change her tune, or I just might drop her in the hands of a vampire that will not be as nice as I am.

"Tatina, you look so worried. Tell me what is going on in that pretty little head of yours," I say. I desperately am trying to sound sympathetic. It is hard when you feel like someone is so damn ungrateful. She is one of the most ungrateful hybrids I have ever had the displeasure of grooming. Why did Craig do this to me?

"I am fine. This place just looks a little creepy. I did not see many vampires growing up even though I have vampires in my family. We mostly stayed to ourselves," she says, looking around at all of the vampires licking their lips and watching her. They want to taste her, but they would never piss off Mr. Craig.

Her innocence, Mr. Craig, will play on that. He will have her eating out of the palm of his hand. She just wants to be loved so badly. She has never had anyone pay her attention. I bet she never sat on her daddy's lap. This little bitch is a trainwreck, and it will be so easy for Mr. Craig to manipulate her right into his plan. She will breed for him willing. I bet I will not have to use a breeding box. She will spread her legs so that he gives her his approval. She will probably want him to watch her breed for him. Could anyone be so stupid?

"Oh darling, I understand, but what I do not understand is why you think I would put you in harm's way. I have been nothing but nice to you. To be honest, this is upsetting me. Mr. Craig told me to feed you and make you happy. You have done nothing but whine and complain. If you tell Mr. Craig I upset you, I will be in trouble. Honestly, you sound ungrateful," I say. I am trying not to come off as a bitch, but I probably did.

She sits there across from me. Looking at me looking at the people in the room.

"I am sorry. I have not been out in the world much, and this is a big city. I will try harder to be grateful. I assure you I am very grateful for you and Mr. Craig," she says, her eyes big and looking a little wet. Maybe she is about to cry. Damn, do not cry.

I scan the room. The vampires are checking her out. I notice one really looking at her. Maybe I will introduce him. I might not be able to handle her after all. Maybe Mr. Craig should just sell her instead of breeding her.

"Excuse me, Tatina. I need to speak with someone. I will be right back. Stay here like a good girl," I say.

I leave the table and her whiny self there. I walk over to the bar. A young vampire with dark hair and dark green eyes is watching me watch him. He smiles like the devil himself when I approach.

"See something you like tall, dark, and handsome," I say.

He stands up from the bar. "Actually, I do," he says.

I reach for his arm. "You are looking at her," I ask.

He smiles. "She looks ripe. Is she?" He asks.

"Mr. Craig will be examining her soon. The auction will be this Saturday at the mansion. She is up for breeding, not sell as of right now, but I will let you know if that changes," I tell him.

I walk away. I knew this was a good idea. They are going to bid like crazy. This one is special. This girl is going to make a lot of money. She probably will not be happy with the way things are going to go down. In the end, she will have everything her little heart desires, and so will I.

I sit back down at the table. Her mood seems to have changed. I hope so. I cannot take it another minute if she starts whining again.

"Feel better?" I ask her.

"Actually, I do. The vampires in here seem okay. Don't get me wrong, a vampire raised me, but I know that there is something about me that they want, and it makes me uneasy sometimes," she says.

I reach for her hand. "My dear, you will be fine. You are under the protection of Mr. Craig. You have absolutely nothing to worry about. He will take care of you," I tell her.

The waitress comes back with two plates and sits one down in front of each of us. Tatina's eyes get really big.

"It's a lot of food, isn't it?" I ask her as I place the red linen in my lap.

She takes her red linen napkin and places it in her lap. "I have never seen so much food. I will never eat all this," she says.

"Whatever you do not eat, I will have them box up. You can give it to the homeless girl we saw on Royal street," I tell her.

The homeless girl. She had to stop and talk to her. Tatina is a very sweet person. I will give her that, but we have things to do. I can't have her out there trying to be a saint. I need her to be ready for Saturday.

"Eat up, Tatina. It won't nourish your frail little body with you staring at it," I tell her.

"Yes, ma'am," Tatina says.

Chapter 9

TATINA POV

Dinner with Lila was ridiculous and a complete disaster. I hope Mr. Craig is not as strange as her. Maybe this is hell and not heaven after all. She just made me uneasy. She seemed preoccupied with something else. Maybe I am worrying too much. It just feels strange to me, and the vampire she spoke with at the restaurant was also very strange. He seemed to be looking at me funny. She thought I did not notice, but I did. Something about all of that did not sit right with me. I will not make the mistake of questioning her again. Next time, I will observe but not question her.

I get to meet Mr. Craig tonight at least there is that for this horrible day. I will freshen up before he gets here and maybe change clothes. I am not sure what I should wear, say, look like, or how to be. I could just try calming down a little and be myself. I am sure everything will be fine. I am just not sure about Lila. The best thing for me to do is keep my mouth shut and listen.

Someone is knocking on my door. "Come in," I say.

"Mr. Craig is home early and waiting for you in the study," she says. I have no idea who she is. She is petite. She is even smaller than me and looks very pregnant. Something about her, glows, almost fairy-like maybe.

"Thank you," I say, but she closes the door before I can even get it all out. She seemed uneasy and stoic. Everyone here is strange.

I run into the bathroom and moisturize my face and apply fresh mascara. What the heck? I put a little lip gloss on. I walk to the door. I feel like I am standing here holding the handle for eternity. I am nervous, but I can do this. Look what all I have already been through in the last few days. I survived the auction. This meeting with Mr. Craig is a cakewalk, and making him happy will come easy to me. I only need to make him happy and be good for him. I can do this, and I will give him whatever he wants, even if it is my virginity. I know I will have to give it to him, hopefully not tonight. I am not sure I am ready.

I walk carefully down the stairs and look around as I go down. I can't remember where the study is located. I think it is that first room. I walk over to the first door. "Not there! Go down, the hall second on the right," I hear Lila yell at me.

I do not even bother saying thank you or piss off. I walk toward the hall. I turn the corner, and he opens it for me as I am just about to open the door. "Hello my dear," he says. Whoa. Mr. Craig is young and handsome. Well, of course, he is young; after all, he is a vampire. I guess I was expecting some creepy guy who wanted a young girl around. I was not expecting this. He is beautiful.

"Hi," I say very timidly.

He reaches for me. "Now, Now. Do not be afraid of me. Come on in here and let us get to know one another," he says, taking my hand and smiling at me.

I take his hand, and he leads me into the study. He sits down in a chair and pats his lap. He wants me to sit in his lap. "Sit right here on me, so I can get a good look at you, my dear," he says.

I do exactly what he says. After all, I do belong to him. "Tatina, you were in a perilous position and there are only a few options for you. Do you understand?" he asks.

"Yes, sir. I am aware," I say.

I am entirely aware that I am in danger, or at least I was, but what about after he is done with me after I pay the debt. Then what? Will I still be in danger?

Craig POV

Damn, she is beautiful. I cannot believe how much she looks like Julie. Jayne said she was a beauty, but she did not tell me she looked like Julie. "Tatina, there are things we have to discuss," I say to her.

She shifts in my lap. "I understand. I was told you have rules to follow. I was told I would be expected to be available to you," she says.

She is so fragile. I am not sure I will ever auction her to breed or auction her. I may keep her for myself. I am sure we could find another breeding bitch to auction. She could be all mine. I could have her with me always.

"I have to ask you something. I need you to be honest with me. It is a little personal?" I say.

She nods. "I know what you are going to ask me, and yes, I am a virgin sir," she says.

"It is important to me that you are a virgin. I wanted a virgin," I tell her.

"I understand. I have never been with anyone in any way. I have never even kissed a boy," she says.

"I understand Horace tried to take something that was not his when you were at the auction house," I ask her.

"Yes. Jayne saved me. She shot at him. He did not take it, but he did try. He almost did, but Jaybe was there. I do not know what would have happened to me. Oh my, I do know, he would have raped me," she says, her words trembling as hard as her petite body.

This poor thing. Damn that Horace, he is dead.

"I will take care of Horace for touching what is mine," I tell her.

She looks me deep in the eyes while listening to my questions. I lean in and kiss her.

"Now you can say you have been kissed," I tell her.

She leans in and kisses me.

"Yes, I can," she says.

She shifts in my lap. Her body is so tiny. I run my hand up her leg just to feel her. I pull her back to me and kiss her again. I haven't really kissed a woman since I lost my Julie. She pulls back. "Are you okay, my sweet?" I ask her.

"Yes," she says. She kisses me and places my hand back on her leg. "Don't stop," she says.

I feel her legs tremble as my hand runs up her inner thigh. "Whenever you are ready for me to stop, say so and I will stop," I say. She is perfect for me. I want her to be all mine. Her breathing is labored, and a slight moan escapes her pretty mouth as I rub her leg. Yes, my sweet, you will be mine in every way I want.

Chapter 10

TATINA POV

Sitting here in his lap with him feeling my body, it is unbelievable. I have never had someone make me feel so good. He kisses me so softly yet so passionately. His hand running up my thigh makes my body tingle and shaky. I am not sure how to react to him. I am not sure what is appropriate. How do I make him feel the correct way? Where should I touch him? I want to touch him. Maybe I am ready for sex.

"Are you okay?" he asks; he gently touches my face and looks into my eyes when he asks me if I am okay. I want to tell him how badly I want him, but I do not want him to think I am a whore. What should I do?

I lay my head on his shoulder as he takes his hand up my inner thigh higher, getting closer to my sweet spot. "I am. I am just a little nervous about what you are doing, but I do not want you to stop," I respond.

He takes his hand closer to my middle. He gently rubs me. "Do not be nervous. I will not hurt you. I will make you feel amazing pleasures," he says.

Something in me tells me I can believe him, but I still need to proceed with caution. "I need to know. I do not mean any disrespect, Mr. Craig. Are you planning to take my virginity tonight?" I ask him.

He takes his hand and gently but firmly rubs me between my legs. It feels so good. He kisses my neck. "I won't do anything you are not ready for, but if you are ready, I will take it from you. It is mine after all, but I want you to say yes, take it," he says.

I lean further into his neck and begin to kiss his neck. "I belong to you. Take what is yours from me, but I have no idea what I am doing. You will have to teach me," I whisper into his ear.

He turns to me and kisses me. He is still rubbing me. "Yes, you do belong to me, but that does not mean I want to take something that you are not ready to give. That is why I wanted your permission. Are you sure you are ready for me? You can say no," he says.

I pull back from him. I look into his eyes and smile. "I would gladly give myself to you. You saved me. I want to be yours," I say.

He slips one arm under my legs and uses the other to support my back. He rises from the chair with me in his arm. I lay my head into him. I feel like a princess being carried by her prince. "Do not worry about anything; I will teach you everything you need to know about being mine," Mr. Craig says.

He carries me into his bedroom. His room is even bigger than mine. He closes the door behind us with his foot and takes me to the bed. He lays me down gently. He returns to lock the door. As he walks back, he starts unbuttoning his shirt. Woah, he is perfect. Why would he ever want me? I am too thin and pale. He is so sexy.

He crawls into the bed beside me. His shirt is off, and I can see every inch of his upper body. I reach out to touch him. He is a gorgeous man. He leans into me and begins kissing me. He takes one hand and starts feeling my breast. It feels amazing. He pushed up my shirt and slides his hand under my bra.

"Take off your top for me, Tatina. I want to see all of you when I fuck you," he says.

I comply and remove my top.

He kisses my breast that is exposed from my bra. He pulls it gently to the side and begins to suckle my right breast, and then moves to my left. He pulls my bra off, breaks the hook, and throws it onto the floor.

He pushes my legs apart and is lying almost on top of me, both of us still in our pants. He begins suckling my breast and nibbling at them with his fangs. It does hurt a little, and I gasp loudly. He kisses down my stomach until he gets to the top of my pants. He unbuttons my pants and pulls at them until he has my pants completely off of me. Here I lay naked in front of him.

I feel so uncomfortable as he removes his pants. He pushes my legs apart further and starts licking me between my legs. He grabs my bottom and pulls me into his face. I moan. I shake. I am so tingly inside. I feel like I could explode onto him.

"Do you want me to stop?" he asks.

"No, sir. I do not. Please do not stop. It feels so good," I moan.

"Good," he says. He continues tasting me. My legs are shaking, and I cannot control my body. He stops.

I open my eyes. He is on top of me. Not inside me yet, but close. "You can still say no. This is your last chance to say no to me. You will be mine in a moment," he says.

I nod to let him know I am ready. He takes his hand and positions himself to enter me. I can feel it. It feels so much bigger than I expected. He pushes into me slowly. I gasp at the sudden pain I am feeling. The pain and pleasure are both amazing and unexpected at this moment. He thrust deep into me. I push up with my body to meet him as he penetrates my body. I grab him tightly. I need something to hold. I need something to help with the pain. The pleasure is fantastic, but his thickness inside me is hard to handle.

I scream and cry out in pain. I cannot help myself. The more I cry, the more he seems to enjoy me. He pushes into me harder now. I cum so hard I feel like I am going to pass out. He leans in and bites my neck as he cums inside me. I can feel him sucking my blood as he cums in me. He lets go of my neck and kisses my ear. "You are all mine now, every inch of you. You can never say no to me ever again. Every inch of you is mine," he says firmly, and then his fangs pierce my neck hard, and he thrusts into me harder as he finishes.

I cannot help myself; I scream as loud as possible and begin to cry.

Chapter 11

Mr. Craig sits on the side of his bed. "You can go back to your room now. I am finished with you for now. GO! Go now," he says.

I gather myself. I am not sure how I feel. I wasn't expecting him to snuggle up to me and tell me he was in love with me, but I wasn't expecting him just to toss me aside either. I should not have cried, but I was afraid, and it hurt so much.

"Yes, sir. I am sorry for crying. I am so sorry I screamed. I am just sorry," I say. I get out of the bed and dress myself quickly. I start to cry again. Why the hell am I crying? No wonder he wants me out of his room. I am probably annoying him. Stop crying!

"Stop that. Stop all of this crying. I am not mad at you. I am mad at myself. I shouldn't have done that with you. It was wrong of me. I am sorry. Go back to your and take a bath. I will come to see you tonight, and we can talk. None of this is on you. It is on me," he says.

"Yes, sir. I am sorry," I say, tears rolling down my face uncontrollably. I cannot stop crying and apologizing. I have to toughen up, or I will never survive.

I go out of his room and walk swiftly to my room. I wonder if he thinks I am a whore. I should've said No. I go into the bathroom and run myself a bath. I slip out of my clothes. I check the water to see if it is hot. I need hot water to wash the whore off of me. Evidently, I just acted like one. I grab some bubbles out of the cabinet. I pour the bubbles into the tub. When the tub is full, I slide into it. I am never getting out of this tub. I totally screwed all of this up. He hates me, and I do not blame him. I hate myself for acting like a whore.

Mr. Craig POV

She was so soft and sweet. I have done some terrible things since Julie died. Hell, I did some terrible things when Julie was alive. I will have to pay someday for the things I have done to the hybrids. Julie too. I am sure she paid for all of the things she did to them. Tatina is beautiful and young. She is frail, but that is not her fault. It is those idiots that raised her fault. She deserves more. Most of the women who land here deserve what happens to them. Not Tatina. She deserves more, and I am going to make things right with her. I want her to be mine. I will not auction her or breed her. She will be my wife.

Lila knocks on my door. "Come in," I say.

"Well, is she ripe and ready to breed?" she asks, smiling. She is just as sadistic as Julie was when she was alive.

"She is, but we are not breeding her. I am going to allow her to stay here. Order another bitch from the auction house. Tatina is mine," I say firmly.

"What?? But she is worth so much. I do not understand. Is it Julie? I know she looks like her, but damn Craig. She is worth a lot of money. Do not let a piece of ass get in the way of making some money off of her. You can keep her, play with her, but damn breed that whore," she asks.

"She is from the same tribe as Julie. She reminds me of her. I am keeping her. If you do not like it well, then you can leave. This is my house and my auction; you can go," I say.

"No, No, No, I understand. She is beautiful, but she is just so tiny and frail. She is so naïve. She needs a lot of training Mr. Craig. She will not be ready for your specific needs quickly, but I am sure we can work it out," Lila says.

"Then we will get her trained up to be my wife. Can you handle that? Can you be in charge of that? Get another girl for our auction on Saturday, but do not let Tatina know what is happening here. She is nothing like Julie. She might look like her and be from the same tribe, but she does not have that dark side Julie had. I cannot take the chance of her leaving me," I say.

"Yes, sir, I will take care of everything just like I always do," Lila says. I know she is mad, but she will get over it.

LILA POV

Great, now I have to get someone to go bid in the damn auction and get a girl here before Saturday. What if there aren't any ripe Fairies in the auction tonight. This is just great. More work for me. I go upstairs to my office. I pull out my laptop and pull up the auction site. I put in Fairy female age 21. I wait for the search to load.

I think I hear crying. I do hear crying. Tatina is crying. I cannot feel sorry for her. I cannot deal with her right now. I have to find a girl for our Saturday night breeder auction. What am I worried about? As soon as she finds out about his breeding business, she will leave him. Maybe if she gets upset with him, then he will sell her. I would love that. I might have to help her find out what he is doing here.

Three girls are available for bidding tonight at the Vampire Authority district three auctions. I will send Jackson. I am going to have him bid on all three just in case Mr. Craig decides to fall in love with another one. I can't deal with this damn crying. I will go check on here after I text Jackson.

I pull out my phone and scroll to Jacksons' number.

VAMPIRE AUTHORITY DISTRICT THREE AUCTION GO TONIGHT!

Chapter 12

LILA POV

Jackson has to text me constantly about the breeders. I should've just gone myself. I have got three days to get another breeder ready for Mr. Craig's auction on Saturday night. I wonder how he plans to explain that to Tatina. She will hate him when she finds out. As soon as she decides she is done with him, I will auction her off. I will put her in a breeder auction, sell her pussy until I am content, and then sell her to that most horrid person I can find just for causing me all of this work. I hate that little bitch!

I believe I can still get a pretty penny for her. He just had to take her virginity, but considering the tribe, she is from, I can still get a lot of money for her. There are not many left from the aurora tribe. My phone is dinging again. I check my phone. Jackson. Damn him. He doesn't have enough sense even to walk around. I wonder if the son of a bitch has help getting dressed in the mornings. The man is foolish.

*Got three. Adeline, Adomele, and Aurora *

Well, finally, the boy did something right. We have to keep them in the basement, far away from Tatina. I cannot have her feeling sorry for them and letting them go. I will let Mr. Craig enjoy her for a while then I will make sure she knows everything he is up to. I will accidentally let one out or open the basement door. I will come up with something and make sure she is home to catch him balls deep in a hybrid.

Tatina POV

I am exhausted. I lay down in my bed. I have cried until I don't think I can cry anymore. I don't understand why he is mad at himself over me. I enjoyed being with him. It was nice to have someone touch me. I want to know why he was upset. I am going to ask him tomorrow. I probably shouldn't, but I need to know. I know I cried, but it was my first time, and I was afraid. I should have held it in until he was done, but it was painful. It hurt so much when he fed on me, but I could get used to it. I just need time, and I need him to be patient with me. I will be good for him.

Enough of this feeling sorry for myself. I am in a beautiful home full of everything my heart could possibly desire. I could text Jayne and ask for her help. Lila said Jayne's number was saved in my new phone. I get out my phone and scroll for Jayne's number. I select her name from the contact list.

Jayne. It is me, Tatina. Mr. Craig got me a phone. I want to talk when you have time

Hopefully, she will get back to me soon. I wait patiently for her response. I take the phone with me to bed. I want to sleep. The phone dings. Thank goodness. I hate to admit I need her help, but I do.

*Hey, Love. I am working the vampire authority auction close by. I will be home tomorrow. I will come by at noon to take you to lunch and show you the city. I will let Craig know. *

I text back. * See you then thank you*

Great. I can get some answers tomorrow. I curl up and close my eyes. I need to rest my body.

Craig POV

I have to apologize to her tomorrow. I know she is heartbroken—my phone dings.

I will be home tomorrow. I will be picking Tatina up at noon for lunch. I hope to see you too

Jayne, she always knows when she is needed. I don't want to see her yet. I will make sure Tatina is ready for Jayne tomorrow. I will go up and apologize to her. I was not very nice to her. I know I hurt her, and I that was not my intention.

I go up the stairs slowly. I have no idea what to say to her when I get up there. I come to her door and knock lightly. She is mine, and I want to be with her, but that is no reason to be a dick to her.

"Tatina, may I come in and talk to you please?" I ask.

She doesn't answer. I turn the door, and it is locked. A good girl, she listens. I take the key to her room out of my pocket. I insert the key and unlock the door. I open the door slowly.

When I go into her room, she is curled up in the bed, asleep. Her face is puffy. She has been crying. I hate that I upset her so much. I brush her hair from her face. I kiss her on the forehead. She opens her eyes and looks at me. She is not scared.

"Hi, Mr. Craig. Are you still mad at me? I did not think you would come to see me tonight, but I am glad you did," she says softly.

I smile at her. "May I lay with you, Tatina?" I ask.

She moves over to make room for me in the bed with her. I gently lay in the bed with her. I wrap my arm around her. I snuggle her. I could lay here next to her forever.

"May I stay here with you all night?" I ask her softly.

"Yes, please stay with me," she says.

"Jayne is coming for you tomorrow. She is taking you to lunch," I say to her.

She snuggles in closer to me. "Okay, I cannot wait to see her," she says.

She drifts off to sleep. I watch her sleep for a while. She is beautiful. I will give her everything. I will give her more than I ever was able to give Julie. She is a light in my dark world. I do not deserve her after everything I have done, but I will love her. Oh, Tatina, I will love you in a way you have never been loved before in your short life.

Chapter 13

I grab my phone to see what time it is. It's 1120. Jayne will be here to get me in 40 minutes. I have not even got up yet. Mr. Craig is no longer in my bed. He snuggled up to me all night. I am not sure when he left, but I know he slept peacefully with me all night. It was wonderful.

I get out of the bed and grab some clothes out of the closet. I dash for the bathroom to get ready. I turn on the shower and quickly get in; I have to hurry. I wash my hair and grab the strawberry body wash. I cannot believe I overslept. I am so excited to see her and tell her everything.

I jump out and throw a towel on my head while I dress. I grab some makeup and try to make myself up. I'm not too fond of makeup but here goes nothing. At least I don't look like a painted-up hooker this time.

I throw on my clothes and give my hair a good drying with the towel. I don't have time to dry it thoroughly. I grab a hair tie and pin it up neatly. I grab some shoes out of the closet and slip into them. I cannot wait to go to lunch with Jayne. Maybe she can tell me more about Mr. Craig and how I can be there for him. I hate to ask her about sex, but I have no one else to talk to about it.

I rush down the stairs to wait on Jayne. I run into Lila. "Is Jayne here yet?" I ask her, smiling. I can tell I am annoying her, but I do not care.

"She is in the study with Mr. Craig," Lila says. She looks mad.

"Okay. I will wait for her here. I don't want to disturb them," I say.

"You and Jayne should spend the night in the city. I will suggest it to Mr. Craig. Jayne can show you some amazing places. She grew up in the city and knows more about New Orleans than I do. Probably more than Mr. Craig," Lila says.

"That sounds great. I would love to if it is okay with Mr. Craig," I say. I wonder why Lila is being friendly to me. She looks annoyed and uneasy but suggests I go have a good time. She is an odd one.

"I am sure he would be happy to see you happy," Lila says. She looks at me with a strange smile. It is almost devious.

Lila pov

This is too easy. If Jayne keeps her in the city, I can get the three new breeders ready and sold before she comes back. Mr. Craig just had to become obsessed with her so quickly. Maybe he will grow tired of her soon before it's too late to breed her. Look at her, ripe and ready to breed, and he is in love with her.

I hurry down the hall to the study. I knock on the door. "Jayne. Mr. Craig," I say through the door.

"Come in," Jayne says.

"Tatina is up and ready. I suggested to her that Jayne and her stay in the city tonight. We are having that party that might be extremely overwhelming to her. Plus, vampires running everywhere. It might not be safe for her here tonight," I say.

Jayne nods, and so does Mr. Craig. He knows she does not need to be here tonight. Jayne is so stupid. How can she not know how Mr. Craig and her sister were. Her sister was a sick twisted bitch.

"I think it's a great idea. What do you think, Jayne? Would you mind entertaining Tatina for a few days? The two of you could have some fun," Mr. Craig says.

"I think it would be wonderful for her. I will make us a reservation," Jayne says.

"No need. I will have Lila call the Bourbon Palace Hotel and make the reservation. I can have one of the guys drive you two in and pick you up in, say, two nights. You want to stay two nights or three nights?" Mr. Craig says.

"That sounds wonderful. I don't have an auction for four days. It would be great to relax, and I could spend some time getting to know her and maybe help her acclimate to her new life. Is there anything I need to help her with? If there is just let me know. Craig, I want the two of you to be happy," Jayne says,

"Why not stay three then," I suggest. I cannot take any more of this. I only want you to be happy bullshit, or how can I help Tatina. It is getting on my last nerve.

"Are you sure?" Jayne asks.

"That would be great for Tatina. You could take her to eat. You girls could walk around the quarter. She would love it," Mr. Craig says.

"I will go make the arrangements and tell Tatina to pack a bag for a few days," I say.

I go back to tell Tatina. This is perfect. It gives me time to get the girls ready without confining them to the basement. I don't have to keep Tatina locked in her room during the auction. She will have to know eventually but not this week. I guess I should let him enjoy her for a while, then I will tell her myself.

"Tatina, go pack a bag for three nights. I have to call the hotel. Jayne will be out in a minute. The two of you are staying in a hotel on Bourbon Street for a few days. She is going to show you the city and take you shopping," I say.

Tatina obeys. She runs straight up to her room to pack while I call the hotel. Shit. I think I hear a car. He cannot be here with the girls already. I run out the door and motion for him to leave. I grab my phone and text him.

Come back in an hour.

I cannot have her seeing all of this just yet. I finish up with the hotel and go to let Mr. Craig and Jayne know. I have to get them out of the house now.

Chapter 14

JAYNE POV

Tatina looks amazing. I am so happy to see her looking so well taken care of with Craig. I was worried a little bit, but she looks great. She was so lost just a few days ago when she landed at the Vampire Authority auction. It makes my heart smile knowing she is in good hands. Craig will be so good to her and for her. I know it.

We load her bags up into my car. "The hotel we are staying in is old but newly renovated and very cool. I think you will enjoy it. It was a nice view of the city. We can sit on the balcony, and people watch and drink, lots of drinking in the city," I tell her.

"Sounds great. I cannot wait. I have a lot to talk to you about that I need help with," Tatina says.

"It is not far. Maybe we will miss the traffic. I will help you any way I can with anything you need," I tell her.

I plan to take her everywhere since we have a few days to explore. "We can go to the French market, grab amazing food, oh and we can ride the ferry and the streetcar. We can walk over to the garden district to look at houses. There is a lot to do. We can go to a few bars. You have got to drink a hurricane," I tell her.

"I have never really had a drink before, but I am excited," she says.

"Well, you are old enough for a drink, and I plan to get you a few. Then we can have that talk," I tell her.

We zip into the city. Just us two girls without a care in the world but the fantastic fun we are about to have. She deserves to have some fun after the way she has lived her life. I want her to be happy.

Lila POV

I did not think they would ever leave. I have my driver driving around three hybrids I need to be checked before the auction. I have emails to send. I have to get this show on the road. There is not a lot of time. I have wasted too much trying to get rid of little miss perfect Jayne and Tatina.

"Mr. Craig, he has the girls and is pulling up with the three of them now," I tell him as I walk into his office.

He looks troubled. I have not seen this look on his face since, well, since Julie died.

"What is the matter?" I ask him.

"I don't think we should do this anymore," he says.

Great, the little tramp has gotten to him. She will ruin everything we have built.

"Really, you're telling me you're going to let a piece of ass get in the way of everything we have built here. You have been doing this for years, and now you are going soft on me all of a sudden. Tatina must have one amazing pussy," I shout at him.

"No, it's not that. I am just tired of it. I want out. I will give you the business. I have money I can set you up. I think it is time for me to move on, and maybe she makes me want to do right. Maybe I should change my ways. I have done a lot of bad things. Julie and I ruined lives," he says.

"Really. I do not have the connections you do. If the Vampire Authority finds out, we are having unauthorized auctions, and it is over for both of us. We have to stick together on this. You cannot abandon me now. Especially over some hybrid whore," I tell him.

Mr. Craig runs his hand through his dark wavy hair and then slams it on the desk. "I am fully aware. That is why I want out. I am ready to have a family. Tatina is perfect to start a family with. Julie and I could never have a family. Now I am getting a second chance. She is sweet and perfect. I want out," he says.

I mean, this romantic sadist, how many women has he assaulted that has come here. He has taken out his rage on them and on me. He has sold them for breeding purposes to vampires to build armies. Some of these women are locked away to breed to multiple vampires for multiple times to the highest bid. He has kept the breeding houses stocked for years, and now all of a sudden, he wants to be in love. Hell no. Not going to happen. I can fix this. I will fix him.

"Fine. We can work out the arrangements, but first, we have to take care of the three women here now. Are you going to check them, or should I?" I ask.

"Do it. Be gentle and do not hurt them. We have hurt enough hybrids over the years," he says.

"Of course, sir. I will be nice. Just like you have always been nice to all of these women," I say.

I storm out of his office and get halfway down the hall. I go back and peck on the door.

"I am sorry for my outburst. It will not happen again," I say.

He shakes his head at me.

I walk back down the hall. I have to get a plan in motion, and I know just the way to do it, but I will need help. I know just the person to take Mr. Craig down. Poor Tatina. Her little heart is going to be so broken. Fuck that whore!

I walk through the main hall and to the side door on the stairwell. Eman has already got the breeders in the basement and locked in chains. Not my usual ideal way to control them, but we don't usually have three women. I cannot risk one of them breaking free and running away. I have got to keep them under control and if I want to take him down. I need these women in the worst possible conditions I can get them in before the auction. They need to hurt, and I am just mad enough to ruin them.

"Eman, bring them water, no food. Then strip them naked redress them in white gowns for the auctions. Before you dress them, I need you to check and see which ones are virgins," I tell him.

"How do I do that?" he asks with a dumb look on his face.

"Idiot!" I yell at him.

"Ram your hand up in there and check for extra skin. I will do it," I scream at him.

The first woman screams, but the other two are silent.

"Look you can behave and let me do my job. After you get food water and a nice quiet afternoon until the auction. Or I can have Eman hold you down and I will do what I need to do anyway, but no food and no water. I will make damn sure you go to the worst bidder we have tonight if you give me any trouble. You want a life of torture then fuck with me," I say to her.

The red-haired freckled face hybrid stops screaming. She acknowledges she will cooperate.

"Good girl," I say to her and give smack on the face.

"Strip them. I will be back in twenty minutes to check them. I need to send out emails. Did you take pictures before you put them in the car?" I ask.

"Yes. I sent you everything in the email. Good. I will need new ones after we dress them. They need to look perfect, so do not punch anyone in the face. If they get out of hand, hit them anywhere but their pretty little faces," I say.

Chapter 15

MR. CRAIG POV

Tonight after the auction, I am ending these auctions. I will turn everything over to Lila. I will tell Jayne everything and come clean. I will be honest with Tatina about everything wrong I have done. Hopefully, she will forgive me and allow me to love her. Something about her makes me want to do right. I have not been right since I lost Julie. I started these breeder auctions, and now, now I know how wrong I was. I was so wrong. I am lying to myself. Julie was just as involved as I was, her death only made me more violent and more of an asshole. I should have stopped then after she died. I was so wrong. I was wrong, and so was Julie. We both deserve hell. I do not deserve Tatina or forgiveness. Maybe Jayne should take Tatina away from me.

Knock at the door.

"Mr. Craig, the three are in the basement. I am getting them prepared. I will send you an email in about an hour with all the information," Lila says.

I acknowledge her. I need out of this. She leaves as I try to console myself.

Losing Julie pushed me over the edge. I became something I should have never evolved into, but I did. I became a crazy person. Tatina, in a single moment, has brought something out of me that I forgot existed. Even if she doesn't forgive me, at least I will be free of all this. I will be myself again. I hope Tatina and Jayne are having a good time. Maybe tonight when all of this is over I will join them in the city. I need to see her and tell her how I feel about her.

Jayne POV

Tatina and I settle into our hotel. I almost forgot how beautiful this hotel is. The last time I was here was with Julie. Now I am here with Tatina. She is a breath of fresh air. I hope she brings out the good in Craig again. He was such a good man. He has become distant since we lost our precious Julie. He loved her so much. I only want happiness for him; that is what Julie would want for Craig. Julie would want Craig happy and thriving, not this beast he has become over the years.

"Tatina, I was thinking we should go for a walk and then grab some food," I say to her as she unpacks her things.

"Sure, I am starving," she says.

She only has a few things. I will change that for her on our little trip. I am going to take her shopping. This girl is going to have a fabulous wardrobe when I return her to Craig. I know he bought her clothes, but damn let the girl live a little.

"Let's go get a drink first," I say to her.

"Sure. No-fuss from me," Tatina says.

"Let us go get something fried and bad for us," I say to her.

"Sounds fantastic," she says.

I unpack my things. I slip out of my heels and into some comfy shoes. No way am I walking in heels. I hope she has comfortable shoes. I pull my hair up into a ponytail. "I am ready. You?" I ask her.

"Yes. I have been ready," she laughs.

I grab my purse, and out we go. We head out of our room and to the elevator. We rush into it, giggling like school children. I pull her close and hug her. "You are going to have a great time miss," I say to her.

"I think so. I am so happy," she says.

We exit the elevator and head for the lobby. The lobby is the same as it always has been: old brick and southern charm. The purples and greens decorate the lobby with street signs from all over the city. It is a unique blend. One thing about this city there is always a unique blend of everything. The food and the culture are beyond unique. We exit the lobby to the street.

"Where to first?" I ask her.

"A drink, I guess," Tatina says.

"I completely agree," I say.

We walk a few blocks to a bar on the corner. The good angel bar. "This is new," I say.

We go in and find a seat at the bar. "Have you ever been to a bar before," I ask her?

"Nope. This is a first for me. I have never been much of anywhere in my life," she says.

"Okay let's get a hurricane and we can chit-chat about everything that has happened since you got in your new home," I say to her.

I order for the both of us. Tatina looks like she is dying to tell me something.

"The bartender is adorable. Don't you think?" I ask Tatina.

"That he is. You should talk to him," she says.

The bartender is adorable. His hair is as long as mine. He has a beautiful smile. "Want me to talk to him for you?" Tatina says to me.

"No, girl. I got this. But tonight I am spending it with you," I tell her.

Tonight is not the night for me to be chasing men. I need to spend time with Tatina at night.

Mr. Sexy bartender brings us back our drinks. "We have good food too, ladies," he says.

I twist about in my barstool. "What do you recommend, Mr. Sexy," I say.

"The house special. It's a sample of our best entrees. It is great. One order would feed both of you," He says.

"Okay sounds good. Bring us that," I say.

"You got it. The name is Russo if you're wondering," he says.

Yes, I was Mr. Sexy.

Tatina laughs as I blush. "I think he has got his eyes on you," she says.

"Well, tonight I am spending with you. I have all the time in the world to hook up," I say.

"So what are we doing after we eat," she asks.

"Probably walk and walk a lot," I tell her.

Mr. Sexy brings us our order. I tap my glass for another one. Tatina has barely drunk any of hers. "You should drink that," I say to her.

"I will, but first I want to eat," she says.

Poor girl has probably eaten more since being with Craig than she ever ate at home.

"So what did you want to talk to me about. Is Craig treating you well?" I ask her.

Tatina begins to blush. Oh, I think I know what this is about. "Jayne, I am a virgin, and I am afraid that I will not make him happy. Well, I am not a virgin anymore," Tatina says.

"You and Mr. Craig have already had sex. How was it?" I ask her. I really thought he would give her some time to acclimate to her new environment. I guess he could not help himself.

"It was odd and good, but he acted strangely and then apologized. I thought he was mad, but then he said he was sorry. I have no idea what I am doing or how to please him," Tatina says.

I take her hand. "Listen, just be patient with Craig and yourself. Girl, it will all come together. Take your time and he will teach you everything he wants you to do to please him. You have to talk to him," I say.

"Thanks, Jayne," Tatina says. She looks like a load has fallen off of her back. That was really bothering her.

As we eat and drink I notice one of the members of the Vampire Authority lurking around. I wonder why they are in town. There are no auctions in this area. Nola is a no auction zone. Someone must be having an illegal auction in the city.

I take out my phone. I message Craig.

Hey, we are having a great time. Is something going on in the city? I just saw VA at a bar

Tatina and I continue eating. Is this guy watching us? When we finish I check my phone. Craig still hasn't messaged me back. Something is off. I get up to go to the bathroom. "Tatina, I will be right back," I say to her. I have to check this out.

As I walk back to the bathroom I notice the VA is following me. "Jayne," I hear from behind me.

I turn around to see Glenn looking dead at me. "Yes," I say.

"We need to talk about Craig," he says.

"I am out with Tatina tonight. Can this wait?" I ask.

"I am going to do you and her a big favor. I know about her background. What hotel are you at?" Glenn asks.

"The Bourbon, wait, what is going on? What did Craig do? Is Tatina in trouble?" I ask.

"I will be there tonight to talk to you. Enjoy your evening. Everything will be fine. Do not message Craig again. I do not want you implicated in all of this. Keep her safe. I need to talk to her. We need her help," Glenn says.

"Tatina?" I ask.

"I will handle it," he says.

Glenn walks out of the bar. What has Craig gotten himself into? What do I tell Tatina? What if Craig messages me?

Chapter 16

LILA POV

Mr. Craig thinks he is going to push me out and have me living in the streets after everything I did for him. When Julie was alive, I did so much for her. I will show him. I made the call, and I will wait. I already have the auction deposits. The vampire authority can seize the bids. I am getting out of here with the deposits and my savings. I know people, and I can set up somewhere else. I can restart my own auction after everything settles. He is going to pay for trying to push me out. Craig will pay, and he will lose his precious Tatina too. Fuck her and him.

I have to check on the girls. The guys are too damn stupid to finish up the auction. When the Vampire authority busts this auction up tonight, I need everything to be perfect. I go down the stairs to see if the idiots gave the girls any food or water.

"How are they?" I ask the idiot.

"I fed all three of them, gave them water, and Ralph checked them. I couldn't do it. I do not like being near them when they are crying and begging. Ralph was happy to do it," Kenu says.

"Well, it sounds like you are on top of it. I can't say that about the other idiots we have working here. What are the results? The little bitches ready to breed?" I ask.

"Oh yeah, all three are ready; all three are still virgins," Kenu says.

"Good. I will update the auction listings. Virgin hybrids equal more money and a bonus for you," I say.

I leave the basement. When the vampire authority gets here and sees these three in the basement, they will arrest Craig. I need to be gone by the time they arrive. I am sure they will wait until the auction is over. I can handle everything remotely. I need to grab a bag and my laptop and get out of here before they arrive. I would love to see Craig when the authority arrests him.

I run upstairs. I grab my laptop, purse, and car keys. I need to get to my apartment to be ready to bolt as soon as the auction is over. I run back down the stairs and out the door. I will have to finish the listings from my apartment. I have two hours until the auction starts.

Tatina POV

I wonder who that strange man was Jayne was talking to, and he seemed odd. It seemed like her entire mood has changed. She seems worried. I hope she is okay.

"You okay," I ask her.

Jayne fumbles through her purse. "Yeah Yeah, I know him from work. Listen, he is going to stop by the hotel later and have a drink with us. He is a super nice guy, so don't be afraid of him. He just looks like he has a stick up his ass, but I promise you he is a good man," Jayne says with a laugh.

"Okay. I love meeting new people. Strange-looking ones," I say.

"Good. Why don't we take our drinks and walk down the street? I need a big drink and something hot to look at," Jayne says.

"Sure, you should see what time Russo gets off work. You could take him to the hotel and show him a good time," I tease Jayne.

"This is my time with you. Man, he is hot, though. Look, we are here a few days so that we can figure it out tomorrow. Maybe I can see him then," Jayne says, smiling and laughing, thinking about the Russo guy.

"Write down your number on the check and give it to him," I say to her.

Jayne takes a pen out of her purse and writes down her number. She slips it to Russo with the check and a big tip.

"Let's go find some music and a little bit of fun," Jayne says.

We grab out hurricanes and walk out of the bar. We exit to the left and walk down to Bourbon Street. We cross over to the other side of the street. I have never seen so many people before. Street performers, fortune tellers, musicians are all out in the street to entertain us. This city is heaven.

"There is a blues bar right down on the left. It is one of my favorites, " Jayne says.

As we walk closer, I see the man from the bar with three other individuals. "Jayne, look, it is that man, and he has friends with him. Is he following us?" I ask Jayne.

"I seriously doubt that. They are probably here on vampire business. Things that do not concern you or me. One thing I learned a long time ago, stay out of vampire business," Jayne says.

"I understand," I say.

I feel like she is hiding something from me. I don't know what, but it's something terrible. "Jayne, you know you can tell me anything; I am not a child," I tell her.

Jayne stops in front of the Blues Bar. "Listen, I cannot go into much because I don't know much. All I know is they are here about Craig. I don't know what, and we won't know until tonight. My friend is coming by to talk to us at the hotel tonight. We will have all the answers then. So until then, until I have to worry until I have to let this be a bad thing, I want us to have fun," Jayne says.

"Okay. Then we should have fun," I say as I open the door to the Blues Bar for Jayne. I follow the sounds of the music straight to the bar. I hope everything is okay. I finally have a home, and now vampires are involved.

"Am I in danger, Jayne?" I ask her.

She touches my face. " I promise that nothing will ever happen to you. I will look out for you for as long as I am alive, and we fairies live a long damn time," Jayne says.

Chapter 17

TATINA POV

Jayne and I arrive back at our hotel. I can't believe how much fun we had tonight. I am worried about Jayne's friend coming to talk to us. I am concerned about Mr. Craig. I have a terrible feeling about Lila. I hope Jayne's friend will be able to help him. I am not sure why I am so worried about him; maybe I should not be concerned. Perhaps I should worry about myself instead of Craig. I cannot be that way, and he did save me after all. I owe him.

"Jayne, is that your friend over there at the bar?" I ask. I point to the man standing in the hotel bar. He is a handsome vampire. Most of the vampires are attractive, but he is beautiful, like Mr. Craig. He does not look as strange looking as he did earlier. Earlier, he gave me the creeps and seemed to be eyeballing me, but now he is intriguing.

Jayne turns to look behind her where I am pointing. "Yes, that is Glenn," she says.

"Should we go talk to him or wait for him to come to talk to us?" I ask.

Jayne looks worried. "Yes, we should. Be careful what you say to him. He is with the vampire authority, and not everyone at the authority can be trusted," she says.

We walk across the lobby to the bar to meet with Jayne's friend, Glenn. He is an older vampire. He fits in, but you can tell he is an old one. The way he moves and looks at me reminds me of the old ones. He is still nice looking, but occasionally he has this odd look; maybe that is his age.

"Good Evening, ladies," Glenn says, his words sliding across his lips, hissing at us. His eyes look me up and down. He is giving me the creeps again.

Jayne and I sit down at the bar with Glenn. "Would you ladies like a drink?" he asks.

"Sure, I will take another hurricane," I say. I do not want him to know that I am the least bit creeped out by him.

"Me, too. That sounds good," Jayne says.

Glenn motions for the bartender and orders us both a hurricane. "We have made some unpleasant discoveries involving Craig and Lila. Are you aware of the auctions he is holding, Jayne?" Glenn asks.

Jayne is stunned. She looks as if she is about to fall off of her chair. She does not know I can tell by the way she is acting. She is upset, and I have no idea how to feel. "What do you mean auctions? He got me from an auction, but he has been nothing but kind to me in the few days I have been with him," I say. I scramble to understand how Mr. Craig could be involved. Lila may be, but not Mr. Craig.

"I don't think Craig is involved in anything like that. Are you sure?" Jayne asks.

Glenn pays the bartender and hands us our drinks. "Lila is trying to throw him under the bus. We know she is involved. She called the authority last night and said she discovered he was auctioning off women to breed with vampires, but we know she is involved with the breeding and the auctions. It seems the two of them have an underground auction and not a good one. It is bad, Jayne, very bad," Glenn says.

"I am bewildered. Then why did he take Tatina. Did he take her to breed? I put her in danger. What have I done?" Jayne is still scrambling to understand.

"I hate to interrupt, but I have to know. Will I be sent back to the auction? I will not run, but please be honest with me. Will I have to go back to that hell?" I ask.

Glenn pats me on the shoulder. "My dear, your debt is paid. However, we could use your help. If you are willing to help the women, Mr. Craig is hurting; we would be grateful in many ways to you," Glenn says, hissing his words again. Vampires, they freak me out sometimes.

"My help? How can I help?" I ask.

Jayne looks as if she is somewhere else. Her face has lost all color. She is visibly upset and distraught. "Craig is such a kind man. My sister and Craig were married for such a long time, and the two of them seemed so happy, and now this," Jayne says. I hate to see her this way.

"Craig may be a good man, but Jayne, he has done some horrible things. At least he was a good man at some point, and you know that, but now not so much. We know something has been off since Julie passed, and we understand he has been through a lot. However, we have rules. Auctions are not allowed outside of the authority and certainly not for breeding purposes. You know fairy breeding is regulated," Glenn says.

"Wait, Fairy breeding? The authority regulates fairy breeding; how?" I ask.

"My dear, Vampires can breed with Fairy to make a very unique vampire breed like yourself. You are a very powerful breed. If you ever tap into it, you will see just what you are capable of, my dear. We keep our eyes on your kind closely. We don't interfere with you unless you get out of hand. It does happen. Fairy vamps require special training and special handling," Glenn says, hissing his words again. He looks at me, almost drooling when talking about breeding.

"What do you mean?" I ask.

"He means the hunger a fairy vamp experiences along with their fairy powers can be dangerous to humans and vampires," Jayne says.

"You know firsthand what can happen, Jayne," Glenn says.

"Let's not bring Julie into this. She is dead and not here to defend herself, so back off of her," Jayne says.

"I meant no disrespect, Jayne. What happened to Julie was tragic," Glenn says.

We sit silently for a moment. Jayne is more distraught. "What will happen to Tatina," Jayne asks.

Glenn smiles and takes a drink from his martini. "You will be her charge for the remainder of her time, just until she has served her term. Then she is free. However, again we could use her help," Glenn says.

"What do you want me to do?" I ask. I have a feeling if I do not help him, I will regret not assisting the vampire authority. I might need his help someday, and it would be better to cooperate with them.

"Simply put, Tatina. I was hoping you could go back to the house and find out what he is doing. We think Lila will probably run if she hasn't already. I plan to act as if we found no wrongdoing, and she will simply return to the house and resume the auction," Glenn says.

"So women will be harmed so you can figure out what is happening. That does not seem right. Shouldn't you stop him? Will anyone be harmed?" I ask.

"No, we will be in place to get them at any auction he and Lila try to have. We have someone in place to get the three he has now," Glenn says.

"Wait, there are women at the house now? There was no one there when I was there that I saw. Is he doing this with me there?" I ask.

"Is that why he had me take her out of the house?" Jayne asks.

"Yes, three breeders he got from an auction just yesterday. I assume that is why he got you out of the house. He is not ready to let you in on his secrets," Glenn says.

"I cannot believe this. What are his plans for Tatina?" Jayne asks.

"We think he plans to keep Tatina. Lucky you did not end up being sold to be bred. It must be because you look like Julie," Glenn says.

"I need another drink," Jayne says. She motions for the bartender.

"I will help you, but I am afraid," I say.

"Tatina, are you sure? You don't have to. You can come with me. The vampire authority can figure this out without you. I promise you they have the resources to do whatever they want to do," Jayne says.

"We can't let this happen, Jayne. We have to help. I have to help. You helped me, and I cannot let this happen to anyone else," I say.

"Oh damn. You are right. But I will be with you. I will take time off work and help you. I will stay in the city and be close, so I can get to you if I need to. You will need to be alone," Jayne says.

"I will make all of the arrangements. We will keep you both safe. Nothing will happen to either of you, I promise," Glenn says.

"I hope you have a good plan," Jayne says.

"We do. We have everything figured out," Glenn says.

Chapter 18

TATINA POV

I thought my life was finally getting better, and here I am, trapped in the middle of something I do not understand, just like the auction. I am scared, but I know I have to be strong. I have to figure out how I can help and just do it. Mr. Craig was so kind to me. Maybe he was only kind to me to get me in bed or to use me for breeding, but that does not make sense. He bought me and owns me. He did not have to be nice to me. He could take whatever he wanted. Maybe he was planning to breed me and get rid of me. Perhaps he needed me compliant and not fussing. I want to cry out and scream, but I cannot. I have to find my strength and make it through this.

Jayne POV

I only wanted to help Tatina and Craig. I thought by suggesting Tatina to Craig, he would see something in her and maybe feel better. I know he has been hurting since Julie died, but nothing excuses this behavior. If he is hurting women, I could never forgive him. My primary purpose will be to help Tatina and make sure she is taken care of and secure her future. She doesn't deserve any of this. She doesn't deserve what her parents did to her or this. She will get the life she deserves. I will see to it. I will take care of her.

I look over at her in the other bed sleeping soundly. I know she is worried. I do not want her to have a single worry. Here we are asking her to go back to the house. How can we ask her to go back into that house knowing what Craig and that damn Lila are doing to women? I will be close, but I cannot be there watching all the time.

We have another day to explore the city. I am sure Glenn will be close by to help prep her for what is to come. I am not sure if I should text Craig or not. He may think it is odd if I do not text him. I will text him later and let him know we are having fun. Maybe he will tell me everything on his own. Perhaps I can help him. Maybe not. I have to do what is suitable for Tatina first and foremost. Should I help him if he tells me the truth? No, I should not. I cannot believe this!

"Jayne," Tatina says softly.

"Yes, sweetie. Are you okay?" I ask.

I get out of the bed and walk over to her bed. I sit on the side of the bed.

"I am scared," Tatina says.

I brush the hair out of her face. "Honey, I am here for you. You do not have to go back into that house. Whatever Craig is mixed up in you can just walk away from it. No one will fault you for walking away," I tell her.

"I cannot let him hurt any more girls. They deserve more than to end up a breeder to some vampire. That could have been me. I could have ended up being raped and breeding babies for some vampire. I cannot let this happen," Tatina says.

How brave she is. How can someone so young be so courageous? "I will be right beside you through this. I will not let anything happen to you," I say.

"I know you will. I do not trust the authority, but I trust you," she says.

"Let's not worry about this right now. I want you to have one day—just one day where you don't have to worry. Tomorrow I am taking on a carriage tour. We are going to have fun and not think about any of this," I say.

"You are too kind to me," Tatina says.

"Get some sleep," I tell her.

She covers herself up, rolls over, and goes back to sleep quickly. What a heavy load for a young woman to have to carry. If Craig hurts her, he will not have to worry about the vampire authority, and I will kill him myself.

My phone rings. I get up from Tatina's bed to check it. I pick it up off the nightstand. It is Craig.

"Hello," I say.

"Hey, I know it's late. I wanted to check on her. I tried to text you, but you did not answer," Craig says.

"We are fine. We went out to eat. We walked around the city. I took her to the Blues Bar. She is having a great time. I am taking her on a carriage tour tomorrow," I say.

I try to sound as normal as possible.

"Great. I knew you would show her a good time. I appreciate you spending time with her. Thank you, Jayne, for sending her to me. I need her more than you will ever know. I think I am in love with her," he says.

"Is everything okay, Craig? You sound a little worried?" I ask.

"No No, No Everything is perfect. She is perfect. I am happy for the first time in a long time," he says.

"I am happy to hear that. I wanted something good to come out of her situation. Listen, I am taking some time off. I want to be close to her while she settles in. Is that okay with you?" I ask.

"Yeah Yeah. I would be happy to have you around. I have not seen much of you since, well since, Julie died. I miss seeing you. I need you around to help Tatina settle," Craig says.

"Craig, I know I have not been around much since Julie died. I want to be here for you now. I think Tatina is good for you," I say.

"I would like that, and I think you are right. She is perfect for me," he says.

"I am going to get some sleep. Tatina and I have a big day tomorrow. I will text you tomorrow. You should come into the city tomorrow night and eat dinner with us," I say.

"I will. Text me the details. I would love to see the city. It has been a while," he says.

"Talk to you then, bye," I say.

I need to look Craig in the eye. I need to see if he is hiding something from me. I need to know. For now, I need to get some sleep so I can make sure Tatina has a good day before she has to go back.

I put my phone back on charge. I pull the covers back and get into the bed. I curl up to go to sleep.

"Goodnight Tatina," I say softly.

Chapter 19

TATINA POV

I can't believe I was able to sleep through the night after everything Glenn told me last night. Jayne seems worried about me. I will be fine. I was almost auctioned into being someone's breeder. How close I came to a life of hell. Now I have to find a way to help the vampire authority stop it. The same people who took me and auctioned me off to pay my father's debts want my help. How is what Craig doing any worse than what they do? They both need to stop. The auction needs to be stopped, period. There has to be someone who cares.

This entire situation is overwhelming. I will find a way to help. What if Craig is innocent? What if it is all Lila? I have to know. I will look him in the eye and ask him.

"Craig is coming to meet us today?" Jayne says.

I continue brushing my hair. Brushing my hair reminds me of when I was little before everything went wrong. My mom would brush my hair and braid it for me. I loved her so much. How could she agree to sell me? Why would any parent sell their child?

"You okay, Tatina?" Jayne asks me.

I stop brushing. I set the brush down.

"I think so. I was thinking about my mother. I have thought a lot this morning about Craig. He is so kind. How could he hurt all of those women?" I say.

Jayne picks up the brush and pulls out a chair. "Sit," she says.

Jayne begins to brush my hair. "My mother would do this for me. I do not know why I was thinking about her today. I should hate her, but I cannot make myself hate her," I say.

"My mother did too. I know you love your family. I know you are worried, but everything will be fine. I promise you," Jayne says.

I lean my head back with every brush stroke. "Thank you for being here with me. You are my family now," I say.

"Tatina, I will be here for you for as long as you need me," she says.

Jayne's phone buzzes.

"Probably Craig wanting to know where we are meeting him," she says.

She walks over to her phone. "It is Craig. What time do you want to meet him?" she asks.

"Soon. I need to look him in the eye and see if it is true. It is eating me alive. I want to know," I say.

"Me too. I have known Craig a long time, and I cannot see him being this horrible person," she says.

"Have him come within the hour. Is he coming to the hotel or meeting us?" I ask.

Jayne thinks for a moment. She finally starts texting him. "I told him to meet us in an hour at the Royale," she says.

"Good. That gives me time to finish getting ready," I say.

"Any ideas about things you want to do today?" she asks.

"I want to walk around it that is okay. Maybe shop. Definitely eat a lot. Maybe get a drink. Will we see Glenn again?" I say.

"Glenn is probably around. He will stay close until this is over. He is the fixer for the authority. Trust me, and he will fix it," she says.

"Tell me about Glenn. You seem to know him well," I say.

Jayne sits down on the bed. I can tell she is searching for her memories. She smiles slightly.

"I have known Glenn longer than I have worked for the authority. Glenn and I are about the same age, to be honest. He knew my family well," she says.

"Oh. So you are friends?" I ask.

Jayne shifts her body. I hit a nerve. "We were very close at one point. He and Julie were very close. Fairies and Vampires have always had a special relationship, as you know. They need us to procreate," she says.

"I do not understand how we can have a baby for a vampire," I say.

"It is our light. Our light can connect with what is left of their human side. We connect with and can give them a child," she says.

"I have never released my light. I do not think I even know how to release it," I say.

"You will. Your mom should've helped you develop your light. That is something I can help you with when you are ready," she says.

"Since I don't know anything about my light, how would they have bred me?" I ask.

"You do not want to know," Jayne says.

"Actually, I do. I want to know what he has done to women who do not know how to release their light," I say.

"Pain. He would cause you great pain either through torture or rape or both," she says.

"Pain? I do not understand," I say.

"It is our defense mechanism. We release light when we are in danger," Jayne says.

"What if the girls he has now don't know how to release their light?" I ask.

"Then he will rape them and torture them until they do and give the vampires the child they want. I have no idea what they are doing with the girls after they breed them and get what they want. Kill them or make them slaves, sell them to another bidder, maybe a slave auction. I do not want to know, but it is important we find out," Jayne says.

"Hell yes, it is. We cannot let this keep going on. This has to stop, but not just the underground auctions; the vampire authority needs to be stopped too," I say.

"You know you cannot just ask him. You are going to have to handle him with care. I think he will tell the truth, but it will have to be on his terms. As far as the authority, I hope one day it will stop," Jayne says.

I pin up my hair and check my makeup. I grab myself something to wear out of my suitcase. I slip into my shoes. "I am ready," I say.

"Well then. Let us get to it. Remember, be easy with him. We need him to tell us everything," Jayne says.

"What if he is innocent?" I ask.

"Then we will help him clear his name and stand by him, but if he is not then we will make sure he goes down for all of this," Jayne says.

"Jayne, I slept with him. He was very gentle," I say.

"Oh, my dear. I know this will be difficult for you. Let's just see what happens today, okay," Jayne says.

"Okay," I say.

I open the door to our room and wait for her in the hall. She grabs her phone and joins me quickly. We begin our walk to the hotel lobby on a mission to find out the truth.

As we walk through the lobby, I see Glenn in the hotel bar. I do not point him out to Jayne. She probably knows he is there. He will be watching the three of us today. I just want the truth. Whatever the truth is, I will accept it.

Chapter 20

CRAIG POV

I gather my things to leave. I didn't tell Jayne, but I booked myself a room at the hotel across the street from the two of them. I plan to make things right. Lila came back this morning as nothing had happened. She thinks I don't know she is trying to expose me and the auction. I offered to give her everything, but now I just want to get this behind me and shut everything down. Before I can do that, I have to tell Tatina and Jayne the truth.

The three women were auctioned off last night, but unfortunately, one of the women was not ready. Draco bought her, and now he is pissed off. I made a deal with him to make sure to get her primed and ready for him. The things that include do not make me feel good about myself. I have to have her ready soon and get her out of the house before Tatina is back home. I need Tatina here with me.

I will play nice with Lila just until we take care of this little problem. As soon as all this is taken care of, Lila is gone. I can take Tatina and maybe we could go somewhere else. We could move far away from all of this and give her a good life. Tatina deserves a good life, but will she love me after I tell her everything.

After I tell Tatina what I have done, she might hate me. It might be better if I am just honest with her as soon as I see her and then give her time to think about things while I clear out the house and settle things with Draco. I should tell her everything from the beginning to the end. I wonder if she will still care for me then? I am assuming she cares for me now. She let me make love to her. I was her first that has to count for something with her. Maybe, just maybe, she will give me a chance to redeem myself.

I walk out the door to my car. I am not even going to tell them I am leaving. They can handle things today without me. I dare not tell them where I am going or when I will be back. Maybe everything will be addressed when I return. I can take care of Draco and shut everything down when I get back. I have to settle up with him, or else he might do something drastic. He has a reputation for being hard to deal with, but he pays cash, and he pays on time.

That poor girl. Maybe I should not leave it to Lila. Perhaps I should handle it. I know what will be required to get her ready. I want to give Tatina all of my attention for today and tonight.

I get in my car and start it—just a short little drive to Tatina.

"Hey, where are you going?" Lila says.

I look at her without rolling down the window, but I do not answer. I put the car in gear and slowly drive out of the driveway.

"Hey. Craig!" She screams.

Fuck! I stop the car and roll down the window.

"What?" I ask.

"Where are you going? We have to settle up with Draco," she says.

"Where I am going is none of your business for one. For two, you work for me bitch. For three I know what you did. Now I have to go. I will be back when I get back bitch. Worry about the bitch in the basement and let me be," I tell her.

"Listen, asshole, and I will take care of it. I will text you if there are problems," she says.

I roll up the window and drive away. She knows where I am going, but it is not any of her concern. I want all of this over before I bring Tatina home. I need to make sure Jayne doesn't know everything, but most of it. In reality, I can only tell the two of them most of the situation. I can never tell either of them everything, no matter how much I want to spill it. If she does, I need to explain to her why and how I am going to fix all of this.

The short drive to the quarter is relaxing. I take my exit and drive under the overpass. I roll down my window to take in the jazz playing. Just a few more minutes until I am at my hotel and Tatina. I miss the city.

I pull into the Valet and wait for the scruffy-looking valet to come to get my car. He takes his time with the car in front of me. He finally walks up to my window to give me my ticket. I grab my bag and exit my car.

I walk through the glass door to the small lobby. I forgot how small the entrance was in this hotel. I approach the desk expecting to wait. The gentleman sees me and waves me forward.

"Mr. Madillion, sir, I have your suite ready," the young clerk says.

I walk up to the desk. "Thank you," I say.

"I put you on the top floor. Unless you would like a suite on the lower floor. The view is outstanding on the higher floors. I gave you the room facing the river," he says.

He hands me a set of keys to my room. I take the keys.

"Thank you," I say.

A bellhop comes to help me with my bags. "Not needed; I only have the one," I say.

I take my bags and go to the elevator. I need to get settled quickly and text Jayne. I hit the button for the 28th floor. I'm not too fond of elevators. It moves swiftly up and dings when I get to my floor.

I step out and walk down the hall to room 2819. I tap my key on the door and open it. I walk through the sitting area to the bedroom and place my bag on the bed. I open the curtains and take in the view. I pull out my phone and text Jayne.

I am here. Where do you want me to meet you two?

I place my phone on the desk to wait for her to text me back. I look out at the river while I wait. It doesn't take her long to text back.

We are on bourbon at the restaurant waiting for you

I text her back *I am on my way. Are you at the cookery?*

She texts back *yes. See you soon*

I put my phone in my pocket and grab my hotel key.

I quickly exit the hotel to get to the cookery to see Jayne and Tatina. I cannot wait to see Tatina again. I hurry down the street. The music is in the air. I don't know why I quit coming into the city. I always loved to go here with Julie. I guess that is why I stopped coming into the city. It reminds me of Julie.

The cookery is only a five-minute walk from my hotel. I have not decided if I am going to tell Tatina I am staying close by or not. Maybe I should. Perhaps she would stay a night with me, and we could talk about our life together and what a piece of shit I am.

I reach the cookery. I walk past the host when I see Tatina and Jayne sitting in the corner. Tatina gets out of her seat and hugs me. Jayne does not. Something is off with her.

"Hey Jayne," I say.

"Hey yourself," she says.

"Tatina, you look wonderful," I say.

"Thanks," she says.

"Have you ordered anything yet," I ask?

"Yes, and we ordered for you too," Jayne says.

"Good, what are our plans for the night?" I ask.

The two shift around, looking at each other oddly. " We have not decided anything yet. Anything interesting going on with you?" Jayne says.

She knows. I wonder how much Tatina knows.

"I don't want to intrude on the time you two have with each other. I know it means a lot to Tatina. I just really wanted to see her," I say.

"Well, I took some time off work to spend it with Tatina. I put in my notice today," Jayne says.

I wave the waitress over. " Gin and Tonic please," I say.

"Something wrong Craig," Jayne asks.

Tatina moves closer to me. "No, everything is fine," I say. It is not fine. I am going to make it okay. But right now, I am in a mess, and I think Jayne knows.

Tatina reaches over and takes my hand. She looks into my eyes and smiles at me. They both know everything. What if it was Jayne who turned me in and not Lila? She sent Tatina here to be with me. Is this all a game? Stop it! She loves me. I know she does.

"Craig?" Tatina says.

I smile at her and try to play it cool. I have to watch the two of them closely. I want to know what they know first.

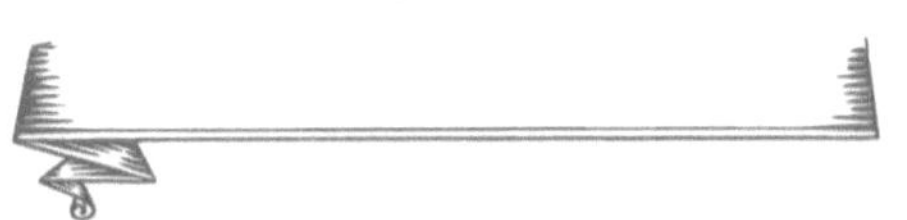

Chapter 21

JAYNE POV

He thinks he is being slick. I wanted to give him the benefit of the doubt, but I can see what he is now. I can see right through him and his lies. Tatina wants him to be innocent, but he is not. I know she wants to be loved, but it will not be by him. I can see why she would need him to be innocent. She wants a better life. When I called Craig and begged him to bid on her, I thought it would be for the best. I had no idea that he already had plans to bid on her. I had no idea he was buying women and selling their wombs to vampires. I will make him pay for all of this.

"So, what do you ladies plan on doing tonight?" Craig asks. His phone is buzzing crazy.

"We haven't really made any yet, but I am sure we could include you if you want to come along," Tatina says.

"I figured we would walk around and see what we could find. I thought I would book a ride on the riverboat. You are welcome to join us, Craig," I say.

"Sounds like fun. You two should go without me. I want Tatina to have fun. I can see her later tonight," Craig says. He looks at his phone. He looks distraught.

"Everything okay," I ask.

"It is Lila. She is handling some business for me today, and I am nervous about it, that is all. She is acting strange lately," he says.

The business, my ass, he is up to no good. They are both acting strange. The two of them are trying to pin all of this on each other, but I see it. I see the two of you.

"What kind of business?" I ask. I do not expect to him to say he is running an auction, but I am curious what he will come up with on a short notice.

"I am closing some of my businesses, and I put Lila in charge of handling it so I can be here with Tatina," Craig says.

Craig reaches for Tatina. She smiles at him. She does care for him. I hate all of this for her, but someday someone perfect will come along for her. I hope that someone is not a vampire.

"I am going to take my drink to go and go to a few shops. Why don't the two of you spend some time together, and I will catch up with you in a little bit?" I suggest.

Tatina jumps at the idea. "Sounds great. I will meet you back at the hotel in a few hours," she says.

I take my drink and leave the cookery. I pull out my phone. I scroll down to Glenn's contact info and hit the message button.

They are alone. Keep an eye on them. Lila is handling something for him today, and I want to know what it is. I am worried about Tatina. Do not let anything happen to her

Craig POV

Jayne leaves Tatina and me alone. That was too easy, and something is up. I feel like she is on to me. As a matter of fact, I know she knows. Tonight may be the only night I get with Tatina. After tonight, it may be over for me.

"I did not tell Jayne, but I got a suite at the hotel across from the bourbon hotel. I wanted to be close to you. I plan to stay there for a week. I extended your and Jayne's room for the week. So we have a week here in the city while Lila wraps up some business for me," I tell her.

Tatina beams with excitement. "Good. We have a lot to talk about. I am so happy you are here with me," she says.

Oh damn, she knows too. Maybe I can explain myself to her. If she will forgive me and my mistakes, then I can start over with her. We can have a good life, but if she is in on it, then I will have to get rid of her.

"Let's eat, and then we can go for a walk," I suggest.

The waitress brings out the food. "Another Gin and Tonic," I tell the waitress.

"Hurricane for me, please," Tatina says.

"Have you and Jayne enjoyed your time here," I ask?

Tatina shifts in her seat. I can tell she is stressed all of a sudden. I wonder what Jayne knows and what she told Tatina.

"Craig, I need to talk to you, but not here. Let's eat and then leave. Don't act any different. I will tell you everything back at your hotel," she says.

I lean over and kiss her. "Sounds good, my love," I say.

She leans over and kisses my ear. "Glenn is watching us," she says. She kisses my cheek and snuggles closer to me.

"I saw him," I say.

I pick up my fork and start feeding her from her plate. We laugh and enjoy our meal. We seem like a normal couple. If Glenn is watching, he will not suspect she is about to tell me everything. I wonder why she is telling me everything. Is that part of the plan? Is she supposed to be on my side or their side?

My phone buzzes again. "Everything okay," Tatina asks.

I look at my phone, and it is Lila again. "She can wait. I am with you now," I say.

We finish up our meal. I pay the waitress and grab us two more to go drinks as we leave the cookery.

"What now?" I ask Tatina.

"I want to go back to your suite," Tatina says. She reaches for my hand. We walk hand in hand down the street, drinking our to-go drinks. It is a short walk back to the hotel. I enjoy every second of it with her.

She doesn't let go the entire walk. She sips her drink and squeezes my hand. As we get to the hotel, she stops at a fishbowl vendor.

"I want one of those before we go up, please," she says.

I reach into my wallet and hand her a twenty-dollar bill to grab her one. I wait on the street while she gets it. I check my phone.

the bitch is being difficult. Call me now

I look up to see what Tatina is doing before I text back.

I will take care of it in a while. Just do what you can. Handle it.

Tatina comes back with her fishbowl. "Lila again?" she asks.

"Yes, I will have to handle it eventually but right now is your time. You are my only concern," I say.

"Okay, good because I want to be all yours," she says.

We walk up to my hotel. I open the door for her to go in. She sips her drink as we walk to the elevator. When we get to the elevator, she pushes the up button and takes a big sip of her drink. She looks back at me, smiles, and kisses me again.

The elevator door opens, and she steps into it. I step in behind and hit the button for my floor. She leans into me. She takes another sip of her drink while we wait. The elevator door opens. I step out, and she follows me. I lead her to my suite. I open the door for her and let her go in first.

"Wow! I think you have a nicer room than us. Not sure that is fair," Tatina says.

"I did not make your reservation. That was Lila," I say.

Tatina sets her fishbowl down and sits down on the couch in the sitting area. "Sit with me," she says.

I sit down beside her. "Tell me what Glenn said to you," I ask her.

She hesitates. "I will, but we have other things to handle first," she says.

She straddles me on the couch. She begins kissing my lips. She is so soft. I run my hands up her back. She starts rocking her hips back on forth on me. I am getting so hard beneath her.

"I want you. I have thought so much about you while I have been away from you. I missed you," she says.

I pull her down to me to kiss her again. I want her. I want every part of her right now. "I want you. I missed you," I say to her.

She continues kissing me and rocking her hips against me. She leans back and slides off of me. She unbuttons and unzips my pants. She pulls my hard cock out of my pants. She looks up at me and then takes me into her mouth.

She is sucking me. I lean my head back and relax, letting her make me feel alive. Tatina makes me want to embrace life again. Right now, I will let her pleasure me. She is beyond exciting. I want to let loose and cum into her mouth. She pulls me out of her mouth and licks the tip of my cock.

"Want more of this, or do you want to fuck me?" she asks. Wow! Where did this come from?

She doesn't give me time to answer. She stands in front of me. I am at complete attention, waiting for her next move. She removes her clothes slowly. I watch her every move. She keeps eye contact with me until the last article of clothing is off of her.

She is in front of me. Her beautiful slender body and nice tits are right in front of me, waiting for me to take her. I want to fuck her.

"I am waiting, Craig. What are you going to do with me? Are you going to fuck me or look at me?" she asks.

I get up from the couch and pull her close to me. I kiss her hard. "Take off your fucking clothes, now," she demands, moaning.

She pushes me away and starts making her way to the bed. I remove my clothes quickly. I join her in the bedroom. She is lying on the bed waiting for me. She opens her legs and closes them back and forth, teasing me.

"Are you going to fuck me or not?" she says.

I join her in the bed. I divide her legs and press my hard cock against her opening. "Tell me you want it," I say to her.

"You know I do. Please give it to me. Fuck me, please, fuck me," she says.

I respond to her request and dive into her hot wet pussy. I pull her legs onto my shoulders so I can go deep inside her.

"Fuck me, hard master," she screams.

I thrust into her hard. She is tight and hot. She feels like heaven.

"Mmmmm, that's it, master, fuck me," she moans.

I give it to her harder and harder.

"Yes, master, make me cum," she moans.

I did not expect her to be this wild. Where did this come from?

She rubs her tits and pushes against me as I thrust into her harder.

"mmm, master, I am about to cum for you," she says.

I cannot hold out much longer. She is so tight and hot. I can't hold out.

"MMMM cum with me, Master," she moans.

Tatina starts shaking as she cums hard. I cum with her as she commands. I love her calling me master, but how did she know that is what I like? Someone told her, and it was not me.

Chapter 22

I lay next to him. I run my fingers across his chest. I want to know. I need to know everything. I am not sure if now is the time to ask, but I am going to ask. Being with him puts me in another state of mind. I am becoming as obsessed with him as he seems to be with me. I just cannot see him hurting anyone.

I look up to him. His eyes are closed. He seems to be resting. I hate to ruin this moment.

"Craig, I have to ask you about the auction you and Lila are involved in? I do not want to ruin this between us. Please, will you tell me everything?" I ask.

He opens his eyes. I can tell he is regretting this conversation. He does not look angry. He almost looks embarrassed, and maybe that he wishes I did not know about it.

"I will tell you everything, but let me explain everything to you before you hate me," he says.

"Did you torture women like me? Have you raped women? I want all of the story and do not sugarcoat any of it. Tell me everything," I say.

Craig sits up in the bed. "It is not a simple story. I am afraid of how you will feel, but if you want to know everything, I will tell you," he says.

"Tell me everything," I say.

"We got involved. Me and Julie because Julie was unable to give me a child. The auction was our way to have a child," he says.

"Julie was involved. Does Jayne know? Is Jayne involved?" I ask.

Craig gets up from the bed and puts his pants on. He goes to the minibar pours himself a drink. "Do you want one?" he asks.

I shake my head no and sit up on the bed. "No, I just want to know what I am getting myself into. But mostly, I want the truth," I say.

"We found out that there are these side auctions we could buy a woman from to have us a child. We brokered a deal. The women would be inseminated with my sperm and have us a child. The deal was she would live with us, and after the child was born we would compensate her greatly. The woman became pregnant, and Julie was happy until things went wrong," he says.

Craig begins to drink.

"Take your time. I can tell this is a lot to go into, and it is hard," I say.

"Tatina, I never meant to lose my wife and our child. I never wanted to hurt anyone," he says.

"I thought Julie was sick," I say.

"Julie did become sick after Elisa came to live with us. She was charming. We basically saved her from hell. Julie treated Elisa like a child. She cared greatly for her and loved her. There became an issue. Artificial insemination would not take. We tried over and over. The doctor advised that I have sex with Elisa to get her pregnant. I did not want to do it. Julie insisted. She wanted a child as much as I did, and this was the only way we could get Elisa pregnant. So now the child would be mine, and Elisa and Julie would not be involved," he says.

Craig is becoming distraught talking about what happened. I let him alone and do not interrupt. I need all of the truth.

"I slept with Elisa. She released her light and became pregnant with my son. Do you know about the light and how a vampire and fairy can have a child?" he says.

"I do not know anything much about my light. I only know what Jayne told me," I answer.

"It is a very spiritual moment. Julie was unable to release her light to become pregnant. Elisa was an answer for us. In the beginning, it was great. Julie talked about helping Elisa so that we could have a big family. BUT Elisa became obsessed with me. She started trying to push Julie out. She started telling me how in love she was with me and how she could give me a family. She started belittling Julie. I became enraged with Elisa. I locked her in the basement until it was time for her to deliver. I know it was wrong, but she was so cruel to Julie. It was affecting her mental state. The two women were fighting. It made the house hard to live in, and all I wanted to do was give Julie a child," he says.

I sit quietly, listening to him. I know this is hard for him. He pours himself another drink. Tears are flowing down his face as he talks about his wife and child.

"Tatina, when my son was born, Elisa went crazy. We offered her money and a home away from us. We offered her everything. She wanted to take the child away. We told her no. She made a deal with us, and she was going to honor it. We allowed her to stay while she was healing. The plan was to move her to the new home I purchased her as soon as she was healed from giving birth. She went crazy that night. She broke out of the basement and murdered the baby right in front of Julie," Craig says.

I sit stunned in silence.

"What happened to her after she killed the baby?" I finally ask.

Craig begins to cry. "Julie killed her. Julie became very sick after all of this happened. She couldn't handle what had happened. She retreated to her bedroom and never came out. The entire thing killed her," he says.

"Jayne knows nothing of this or what happened?" I ask.

He shakes his head. "No, Julie did not want her to know how we got a baby. She was going to keep the entire process a secret. After Julie died, I was furious, and I became deeply involved with these auctions.

I started auctioning off these women mostly to Draco. I guess it was something to keep me occupied. Yes, I did horrible things after losing my wife. I am sorry for it. I want out," he says.

"Why did you hurt all of those women?" I ask.

"I saw Elisa in all of them. I saw how that bitch destroyed my life. Then something changed, and I wanted out. I know Lila turned me in when I told her I wanted out, and now she is back, acting like everything is okay when her plan didn't go how she thought it was going to go. I know Glenn is here watching me. Just when I think I might be able to be happy again," he says.

"Why do you think you can be happy now?" I ask.

Craig sets down his drink and rushes to me. He kneels between my bare legs and kisses my stomach.

"Because of you. I know we can be happy together," he says.

I place my hand on the back of his head. I begin softly, running my fingers through his hair. He has his head lying on my naked body. I feel bad for this poor man, but it doesn't excuse the horrible things he has done.

"Why me?" I ask.

Craig looks up at me. "You make me want to do good again," he says.

I want to believe him. I want to believe in him. I want to help him.

"Glenn asked me to go back to the house with you and find out if you are still participating in the auctions," I tell him.

"I have one woman at the house. If I don't get her ready for Draco, he will kill me. I have to handle her, and then I can get out. We can be together," he says.

I continue rubbing his head. "I will help you, but you cannot hurt her. Promise you will not hurt her," I say.

"Lila is with her. She said the girl is being difficult and refusing to give Draco what he wants," he says.

"I will go back with you and talk to her. I will help you, but you have to get out. Promise me this is over," I say.

He looks up at me and nods his head. "I promise you it is over," he says.

I look into his eyes. I so desperately want him to be telling the truth, but what if it is a lie.

Chapter 23

TATINA POV

I stayed with Craig all night. I plan to go back with him today and help him tie up all the loose ends. I believe him. I believe he wants out. I want to help him put all of this behind him. The two of us can move on and build a life together.

"I texted Jayne and told her you are with me. I do not want her to worry about you," he says.

I pull the covers up over me tighter. "Good, I do not want her to worry about me. She cares a lot about me and you too. She is worried about you," I say.

Craig sits on the side of the bed. He begins brushing my arm softly. "You are too good for me. I am not sure I deserved you, Tatina," he says.

I rise up to kiss him. "I don't know about that. Maybe we can be good to each other. We can build a life and deserve each other," I say.

I rub his arm softly. I lean in to kiss him. He meets my lips and gently nibbles at my bottom lip.

"I want you again and again and again until you cannot handle it anymore," he says.

I kiss his neck and whisper in his ear. "How bad do you want me?"

He pushes me back onto the bed. He pulls the covers back to expose my naked body. He runs his fingers across my lips, down my chest, and begins rubbing my breast. He grabs my breast and leans in to kiss me again. He continues caressing my body. His hand explores me.

Down my stomach and in between my legs, his touch is heavenly. He grabs me in between my legs roughly, and I moan.

"I said I want you. Tell me you want me," he says.

I squirm as he touches my body, staking his claim on me. He can have me, and he knows he can have me. I love him. I do not know why but I am in love with him. "I want you, Master," I moan.

"Show me how bad you want me," I say.

Craig joins me on the bed. He divides my legs and positions himself to feast on me. He begins licking me between my legs. His tongue is a divine instrument pushing me to a limit I was unaware I had. He devours my pussy. Licking and suckling me as I moan and squirm beneath him.

"Do not stop, Master," I command.

He has both of his hands under my ass, squeezing me and pulling me into his mouth. As he slips his tongue inside me over and over, I feel as if I am going to explode all over his face. I moan so loud as he devours me.

Just when I feel as if I am about to explode, he stops. I look up to see him over me with his hard cock at my entrance.

"Fuck me hard, Master," I scream.

His hard cock dives into me with blunt force. I feel as if I am going to split into from the tremendous member diving into me.

"Harder, Master. I want it hard," I moan.

He doesn't disappoint. He gives it to me harder and harder. He is filling me completely. My walls are tingling from the force of his hard cock taking me hard.

He comes closer to me, and I can see his fangs. "Drink from me while you're fucking me, Master," I demand.

Craig sinks his fangs into my neck, drinking from me as he destroys my pussy with his hard cock. My entire body is tingling, but I want something more, and I am afraid to ask.

"Tell me what you want," he says.

I moan, but I do not answer. He begins drinking from me again. I squirm and push up, meeting his thrust. He stops drinking from me and asks again.

"Tell me what it is you are wanting," he demands.

I push him up and look into his eyes.

"I want..... ummmm... I want you to....," I scramble to tell him.

He thrust into me hard as if he was punishing me for stammering.

"Tell me now. Do as your master commands you," he commands.

"I want you to fuck my," I try to tell him.

He thrust into me harder and harder.

"Tell me now," He demands.

"I want you to fuck my ass," I finally tell him.

He smiles. He knew what I wanted. He just wanted to hear it from me. He pulls out of my hot wet pussy and starts teasing my ass with his hard cock.

"Tell me again," he demands.

"I want you to fuck my ass, Master," I say meekly.

He starts positioning himself to give me what I am asking for. He is teasing me, rubbing his huge cock against me. Rubbing harder and pushing just the tip inside my ass.

"I will be easy at first; just relax princess," he says.

I relax my body. I am tingling from the excitement.

"I want it, Master," I say.

"Just relax," he says.

He slides into me just a little, rubbing my clit as he slides carefully into my ass. As he enters, he takes his fingers and slides two inside my pussy. He is rubbing my clit with one hand and has two fingers inside my pussy while sliding carefully into my ass. The pleasure and the slight pain are euphoric.

"I want it so bad, Master," I demand.

He pushes into me, finally giving me what I want. I moan and cum hard as he fucks my ass.

He leans into me and begins suckling my neck again. His hard cock in my ass and his fangs in my neck. I can feel myself tingling. I am going to cum again.

"Harder, Master," I demand.

He plows into me harder. I do not want this to end. I love how he fucks me.

"Is this what you want?" he asks.

"Yes!" I moan.

"Cum again," he demands.

I cum hard again. He pulls out of my ass and spews his hot juice all over my mound.

"Good girl," he says.

He lies down beside me. He pushes my hair away from my neck and begins drinking from me again. He pulls me close to him. Our naked bodies touch as he drinks from my neck. He takes his hand and begins fingering my already tingling pussy.

"Want me to make you cum again," he asks.

"Mmmmm, yes, Master," I answer.

My back to him, his fangs in my neck, his fingers pounding my hot pussy, I can feel him behind me, so hard and eager to fuck me again.

"Cum for me again. Cum for your master," he demands.

I obey and cum again all over his fingers.

He kisses my neck. "I love you," he says.

"I love you too, Master," I answer.

"Your master will take care of you forever," Craig says, kissing my neck and then feeding from me again. I love him so much. He is so perfect.

Chapter 24

TATINA POV

I get up before Craig. I need to go over to the hotel and talk to Jayne before I leave with him. I slip into my clothes quickly. I gather my phone and purse. I need to tell Jayne everything. I want her to know that Craig is not a bad guy.

I rush over to him in the bed. I lean in to kiss him. He grabs my arm. "Where do you think you are going?" he says.

"I am going to get my bag and talk to Jayne before we leave. I did not mean to wake you. I am sorry," I say.

He sits up in the bed. "I can send someone to get your bag. You do not have to get out. I can take care of everything. Get back into the bed," he says, slurring his words at me.

"I know you can. I did want to talk to Jayne before we left. That is all. I wanted to tell her how much fun I am having, and I wanted to thank her for everything," I say.

He points to my phone, "Just call her. You can talk to her in front of me unless you are hiding something," he says.

"Craig, she has been so kind to me. Don't you think I should tell her bye? This would be rude of me to treat her this way. Why are you being this way?" I ask him. I do not understand what is going on with him. I want to help him, but he is acting crazy.

He relaxes. "You are right. Do you want me to go with you?" he asks.

"If you want. That would be great. We could go to breakfast or something," I say.

"No No No, go ahead. I will order you breakfast for here. So hurry back to me," he says.

I lean in and kiss him. What in the hell has gotten into him? He pulls me close to him. "You are mine, Tatina. Do not forget who your Master is or what you are to me," he says.

I smile. "I know I am yours," I respond.

I calmly leave the room. When I am out, I run for the elevator. I need to get to Jayne. I cannot get to our hotel quickly enough. Something is wrong with him. He is not acting right.

When I get to our room, I unlock the door. Jayne and Glenn are waiting for me. "Are you okay?" Jayne asks.

"I think so. He is being really weird. He did not want me to come back to see you. He wanted to send someone for my things. He grabbed my arm and just started being possessive, but then he backed down," I say.

Glenn and Jayne looked at each other. Jayne rushed to my side. "You do not have to go to the house," she says.

I sit down on the bed. "He told me about Julie, he told me about the breeder for their child. Did you know?" I ask.

"Yes, I knew about what they did and about the murder," she says.

"This is all very confusing to me. I do not understand why he blames our kind for what happened to him. I never hurt him, and I been nothing but sweet to him. I was really sweet to him last night, and now he is insane," I say.

Glenn approaches me. "Tatina, what you are doing is dangerous. You have to be careful with him. Do not let him think you are helping us. Try to keep your distance. Absolutely do not sleep with him or let him drink your blood. Do you understand how dangerous this is for you?" Glenn asks me.

I nod my head. "I do. He told me there is one girl there and that she is being difficult. He told me that Draco is who she is promised to, he bought her. He said he would handle her. He also said Lila was handling her now," I say.

"They are probably torturing the poor woman to get her light," Glenn says.

"Are you sure you can go back? You do not have to go back. We can figure out something that does not involve you," Jayne says.

"No, I want to help. I need to know everything," I say.

I begin to gather my things.

"Give me your phone," Glenn says.

Glenn takes my number and programs a number on my phone. "I put an emergency number in your phone; it is under the spa. Just call it and hang up if you need me. I will trace it and be to you immediately," Glenn says.

I shake my head. "I will be fine. I do not think he will hurt me as long as he thinks I am his," I say.

Jayne helps me pack the last few things I brought with me. She hugs me. "Everything will be fine. I will be close, and I will be coming to the house to check on you a lot until this is over. If they refuse to let me in, I will call Glenn," she says.

"I am going to walk her out," Glenn says.

Glenn opens the door for me and follows me out into the hall. "Did you do everything I told you to do last night," he asks.

"Yes, sir, I did," I say.

"Good girl. He will follow you to the end of the earth if you keep it up. We will take care of the rest," he says.

This entire thing makes me feel dirty. I am not sure which one of these people I can trust. Jayne. I know I can trust Jayne. Glenn and Craig both are making me feel unsafe. I feel for Craig and what happened, but how could he hurt these women. I need more answers.

I rush back to Craig. I do not need him upset because I took too long. He is being really strange towards me this morning.

When I get back to the room, he is waiting for me with my breakfast.

"Pancakes!" I exclaim.

Craig smiles a big smile. "Last night, you said you had not had pancakes in a very long time, so I ordered you banana pancakes and maple syrup," he says.

I sit down in front of my plate. "I cannot believe you did this for me," I say.

He sits down beside me. He takes my plate and begins cutting my pancakes for me. Okay, this is strange. He puts butter and syrup on the pancakes for me. He takes my fork and scoops up a piece of pancake.

"Open wide and let your master feed you," he says.

I open my mouth, and he begins feeding me.

"Good girl. Your Master will take care of you in every way, Tatina," he says.

"I can feed myself, sweetie," I say.

"No, Master wants to feed you and bathe you and maybe fuck you raw this morning," he says.

Holy fuck, what is going on? Glenn said this little routine would work on him, but I was not expecting this. Glenn told me to call him Master that it was his kink.

"Yes, sir," I respond.

"Good girl. Master likes a good girl," he says.

I place my hands in my lap and let him feed me my breakfast.

"Now, let me give you a bath and get you dressed properly before we head home. I want to take care of you, Tatina. Remember, you are mine always," he says.

"Yes sir. I mean Master. I belong to my Master," I say.

I get up from the table and go to my bag to get some clothes.

"No, I brought you something to wear for just for your master," he says.

"Yes sir," I say.

I go into the bathroom to wait for him.

He comes into the bathroom with a pink dress and slip-on shoes. There is a collar and a chain for my neck. He plans to treat me like a pet. I am his slave. He turns on the water in the shower.

"Get in for master," he says.

I step into the shower. He takes the soap and begins to bathe me. He washed every inch of me.

"You are such a good girl. Now step out for Master. So I can dry you off and get you ready," he says.

I step out of the shower. He towels me off. He towels me softly except when he towels my pussy. He is rough with the towel. I do not say anything. I let him do whatever he wants.

He takes the pink dress off of the hanger and slips it over my head. He hands me white cotton panties to slip into. He then places the shoes in front of me.

"Now you look like my little slave fairy," he says.

"Thank you, Master," I say.

"Do you know what slave fairies do?" Craig asks.

I look him in the eyes. "They serve their master without asking any questions," I answer him. He smiles. This is what he wanted to hear.

Chapter 25

I adjust the collar around her neck. She looks perfect as my little slave. I love her and want her to be mine and only mine. I will not share her with anyone, not even Jayne. I will take her far away and hide her from the world. It will be just her and I. I cannot trust that Glenn will not try to take her from me. We have to run.

I help my little fairy slave into the car. I tip the valet and take the keys. It is time to take her home. I have to handle the bitches at the house. I have to get rid of Lila and the other Fairy. Then and only then can I start my life with Tatina. I wonder why she started playing this little game with me so easily. She came into my bed and said all the things I wanted to hear. I hope she isn't deceiving me.

I get into the car. I reach over and buckle her seatbelt. "Safety, my sweetie," I say.

She smiles as I buckle her seatbelt. She has not really said much. She has followed me around and done as she is told. I like this. No, I love it—my little fairy slave. I love having her on a leash and pulling her around to bend to my will.

I look over, and she is sleeping soundly. Yes, rest up, sweetie. Master has big plans for you tonight. Big Big plans. If I have to, I will drug her again while I get rid of the other two. I do not need her interfering in everything I have to do so we can leave.

As we pull into the driveway, I hear her phone buzz. I reach over and take it from her hand. It's a text from Jayne.

enjoyed our time. See you soon. Love you

I will tell her about the text when she wakes up. The bitch Lila is running out to meet us. I park the car in the front and get out quietly.

"Do not wake her," I say to Lila.

Lila is visibly distraught. "Draco has been here, and he is coming to get his purchase later. He is pissed off you were not here. The damn fairy is acting insane toward him," she says.

"Grab Tatina's bag and go make her lunch. I will handle the Fairy," I say.

Lila does as she is told. She knows if this doesn't go right, Draco will take it out on her first. He is a mean vampire. He is not allowed to bid in vampire authority auctions. It always worked out for me. He is one of my best customers. He buys all the hybrids I can get my hands on, and he pays top dollar in cash.

"What are you going to do?" she asks.

"Did you try the box?" I ask.

I can tell it is a no from the look on her face. "Get one of the idiots to get the breeding box out. That should do it," I demand.

"Do you want me to make lunch for Tatina or get the box? I can only do one or the other. Which one do you want me to do first?" she asks.

She is infuriating me. "Multitask. You have a phone. Text one of the idiots to set up the box in the basement while you make Tatina's lunch. Can you handle that bitch?" I ask.

Lila shakes her head yes. What a stupid woman. She just thought she could get one over me. She is done. As soon as this is over, she is done. I will strangle the life out of her.

"Yes, sir," she responds. She takes Tatina's bags and leaves with her head down.

I open the car door. I unbuckle Tatina's seatbelt. I gently pick her up out of the car. She is so sleepy. It must be the little something extra I put in her pancakes.

"Sleepy girl you are, but master needs you to sleep right now, my love. Just sleep. I will carry you to your room," I say.

I carry her gently into the house. This house better be quiet so she can sleep. I will not allow disturbances. I do not need her coming down the stairs and running into Draco or a fairy strapped to a breeding box.

I carry up the stairs. Lila left her door open and turned back the covers for her. I lay her on the bed gently and cover her up. I kiss her forehead.

"Thank you, Master," she says.

"Just sleep, my love. I will be back soon, and we will play," I say.

I put her phone beside her bed and plug it in to charge. She looks so sweet sleeping. I would love to stay here with her, but I have to take care of the bitch in the basement.

I close her door and lock her in her room. If she does wake, I do not need her leaving her room. I rush down the stairs to the kitchen to check on Lila.

"Did you tell the idiots to set up the box?" I ask.

Lila is cooking for Tatina. "Yes. I will have her lunch ready in thirty minutes, and the idiots are setting up the box," she says.

"Good. I will be back by then to take care of her. She is locked in her room. Do not let anyone in the house, especially Jayne," I instruct her.

Now to handle the bitch in the basement. I unlock the door to the basement. I can already hear the bitch screaming.

"Please let me go," she screams.

I open the door to the room she is being held in. When she sees me, she stops screaming. "Can you help me, please?" she asks.

I walk over to her. "You are stunning. Draco is very upset with you. How can we solve this problem?" I ask her.

"I just want to go home. Please let me go home," she says.

"As soon as you give Draco what he wants, you can. From what I understand, you have nowhere to go. Draco is offering you a place to live and money. Why are you being difficult?" I ask.

"I don't want him touching me. I know what he wants. He wants my light," she sobs.

"Bring in the box," I tell the idiot.

One of Lila's henchmen leaves the room and rolls in the box. It is wooden and built for difficult fairies. It makes it easy to breed with them when they are unruly.

"I hate it has come to this dear, but this is what is going to happen. I am going to give you a shot to make you manageable. Then that idiot and I will put you in that box over there. Your hands and legs will be tied. It will be painful. Then Draco will have full access to whatever he wants from you, or you can quit being a bitch lay back and spread those legs of yours and let him fuck you. So what is it going to be?" I ask

She starts sobbing. She is not going to cooperate. I step into the closet. I pull out a syringe and draw up a shot. I put it in my pocket. I walk to the bed she where she is chained up. I reach for her.

"Now, Now. It will be okay. I am going to make this easy for you," I say.

As she sobs into my chest, I take the shot out of my pocket and stick it into her leg. "Put her in the box and call Draco. Tell him the bitch is ready to breed," I say.

I hand the syringe to the idiot and leave the room. I have a lunch date with my little slave fairy. At the end of the day, I plan to be far away from here with Tatina.

Chapter 26

TATINA POV

I wake up groggy. I have such a fog in my head. I think he might have drugged me. I do not know why. I was being cooperative. I am doing just as Glenn told me to do. Now, he is drugging me. Why would he do that to me?

When Glenn took me aside, he told me to let Craig baby me. I have never heard of such a thing. He told me to call Craig Master that he would eat it up. How does Glenn know these things, I wonder? I probably do not want to know. Today I have to figure out how to get to the basement and get the woman and myself out of here. I am so out of it that I cannot help myself out of here, much less anyone else.

I try to move, but I cannot. What in the hell did he give me. I hear noise and the unlocking of my door. Did he lock me in here? That jerk. I lie still and wait for him to come into the room. He walks in quietly. He sits a tray down on the table.

"Tatina, my love, it is time to wake. You need to eat. Please wake and eat for master and then master is going to fuck you," he says.

Why is this idiot talking to me like that? What a strange man! How I wanted him to be good and be able to have a life with him, but no. This doesn't seem right. Okay, Tatina, calm down and just go with it. I rub my eyes and stir a little.

"I am so hungry, master. Please feed me," I say.

He pulls back the cover. I reach for him. This is so stupid. He picks me up. I wrap my legs around him. He carries me and sits me at the table.

"Let me cut this up for you. I will feed you, and then we can talk," he says.

I nod in agreement. I am not sure if I should just let him take care of me or say anything. I am so lost. This man has lost his damn mind. I wonder if Glenn ever filled Jayne in on all this bullshit. He did not want her to know everything yet.

Craig begins cutting up my food and feeding me.

"You got to eat now, sweet girl. I need you healthy so you can have me a baby. My sweet fairy slave will have a lot of babies for me. We will have a huge family," he says.

No, sir, we will not have any children, and I no longer feel sorry for your crazy ass. This is going to be over soon.

"A baby, Master. I cannot believe that my master wants a baby with me," I say, smiling.

"Yes. I want a baby with you, Tatina. I want a lot of babies," he says.

"Can I ask you, something Master?" I ask.

"Sure, are you confused about all of this? Why do I like this? Why do I want you to be my slave?" he asks.

"Yes, Why?" I ask.

"When you called me Master in bed, it reminded me of all the games I played with Julie and our lifestyle. I want that with you. You do not have to be my slave all of the time,e but I really wish you would do this for me and let me have this moment," he says.

"I can do that for you. I want to make you happy. Is everything else under control?" I ask.

He cuts his eyes at me. I have asked something he did not want me to. "The other is being taken care of, I promise. When it is over, we can have a wonderful life together. Me, you and our children," he says.

"Okay. That is all I want. I want a life with you," I say.

He begins feeding me again. "I am really getting full, Craig," I say.

"Do not call me that. You call me Master or Master will punish you," he says.

"Punish me. You want to hit me," I inquire.

"If you are bad, I will. So I suggest you be a good little slave for me," he says.

How can he just flip like that? One minute he is so sweet, then he turns into a jerk.

"Yes, sir, I understand. It would help if you told me the rules," I suggest.

"You will be with me always, or you will be locked in this room. You cannot go anywhere without an escort: no bathing yourself and no feeding yourself. You will not do anything without asking me first. No visitors without my approval, and that includes Jayne," he says.

"No, Jayne. Why?" I ask.

"No questioning me either. You are mine," he says sternly.

"Then are you mine also, Master," I ask.

"Yes, my sweet love. We belong to each other from now on. It will be just me and you," he says.

"What about Lila?" I ask.

"She will be gone very soon," he says.

I almost felt sorry for this man. I wanted to help him. I do not anymore. I want away from him. Maybe this was a bad idea.

"Do I have a choice in all of this, Craig," I asked?

Craig becomes furious. "I paid for you. You are mine. Never call me Craig again. I am your fucking master. Your body belongs to me," he says.

He stops feeding me. He picks me up from the table and carries me to the bathroom.

"Bath time," he says.

"I do not need a bath. I had a shower earlier," I say.

"I said it is bath time, bitch," he says.

He begins running water in the tub. He fills it with warm water and bubbles. Seriously bubbles.

He undresses me and picks me up. "I can step in the tub by myself," I say.

"Why the smart mouth all of a sudden?" He asks.

He puts me in the tub. I sit quietly. I am pissed off now. I am not sure I can handle this. He begins washing my body. I sit. I refuse to move. I am going to make him work for this. If I end up stuck in this situation, I am not going to make it easy for him.

He picks me up out of the tub and begins to towel me off. He pushes me down in the chair naked with the towel barely covering me. He starts brushing my hair roughly.

"I cannot tolerate a smart mouth, Tatina. I can beat that smartass mouth out of you. I have a belt, and I will; just on your bare ass, just try me," he says.

I do not acknowledge him. This infuriates him. Good. Now we are both mad.

"Stand up," he says.

I stand up from the chair. He places his hand on my back and forces me over the counter. He takes the hairbrush he has been brushing my hair with and smacks my bottom repeatedly.

"Stop, that hurts," I say.

"Take it, slave," Craig screams at me. My ass is stinging as he hits me over and over.

"Stop, you are hurting me!" I scream.

"Good. You will remember that the next time you decide to question me," he says.

"You cannot be hitting me," I say.

He smacks me again. This time harder. My bottom is burning from the impact of the hairbrush on my bare skin.

He reaches into his pocket and pulls out a shot. He sticks it into my arm.

"Until you can behave, I will have to give you medicine every day to ensure you do," he says.

He is drugging me. That is why I am so dizzy. How am I going to escape if I am drugged?

He picks me up and carries me to bed. I can feel his hands all over me. He is going to rape me.

"All of this is mine. Do not forget it. You are mine. Every inch of you belongs to me. Every hole is mine," he says.

I feel him slipping a shirt over my head and something plastic under me. He is putting something plastic over me or on me. I am not sure what it is—you sick twisted man. I try to fight, but I cannot move. Sleep. I believe I will just sleep.

Chapter 27

CRAIG POV

I leave my angel sleeping. This is going to be difficult. I thought by the things she was saying in bed the other night that this was what she wanted. Maybe I can convince her to give me what I want. I want her to be mine.

I need her to be my fairy slave, just like Julie and I played before everything went wrong. I need her to want it too. I need her. She makes me want to be with her and only her.

I wonder what exactly Glenn told her. I will ask her while she is still drugged. Maybe I can get the truth from her. I hated having to punish, but she needs to learn that I am the only person who will look out for her.

I have to get rid of Lila and Jayne. I am sorry, Jayne, but you have got to go. You cannot be a part of this. I know Julie told you some things, but you cannot be a part of the things that are to come. I cannot risk losing Tatina.

Now to take care of Draco, Lila, and the bitch in the basement. I rush down to the basement to check on things. I do not hear any screaming, so she must be out. I may need to give her an extra shot before Draco gets here.

I open the door to find both the idiots in the room with her.

"Any word from Draco?" I ask Lila.

She nods her head. Emno is standing over the woman.

"You better not touch her," I say.

"I won't. I know better. I do not want Draco killing me over fairy pussy. It is not worth it," he says.

The woman is locked into the breeding box, ready for Draco. "Give her another shot. I do not want to take any chances with this going bad," I tell Lila.

Lila looks at me like I am stupid. "Are you sure? We have already dosed her again?" she asks.

"Yes. I do not understand why you needed me here for this anyway. Why did you two not just dose her and put her in the box yesterday?" I ask.

The two idiots look at each other. "You did not think to make it simple, did you? Or could you just not stand me being in the city with Tatina?" I ask.

"We were not sure if we should dose her and use the box after what happened last time," Lila says.

"That was an accident. Besides, Draco wants her for his personal slave breeder. He is going to have to get her to submit. The box and the shots should do it," I say.

"He is keeping her. I thought he was just breeding her," Lila says.

"It really is not any of your business, is it, Lila," I say.

"I guess not," Lila says.

Lila's phone buzzes. She looks at it.

"It is Draco. He is here," she says.

"Send the idiot up to get him. I will stay here with the woman," I say.

The idiot leaves and goes up the stairs to retrieve Draco. This should make him happy. At least now he can get her to submit.

The idiot returns with Draco. Lila and I did not even look at each other. She knows she messed this up. The last auction I wanted to do, and I think she is messing this up on purpose.

"This is much better. That bitch has some fight in her," Draco says.

I laugh. "She doesn't now. She is ready to submit to you," I tell him.

"Why did these two not do this already? I could be on my way home with her already," he says.

"You know good help is hard to find. You can borrow my box. Hell, you can keep it. I do not think I will need it again," I tell him.

"Yes, I will need it for a while. The two of us are going to make an army of hybrids. Is she drugged?" he says.

"I am sorry it took so long to get her straight. I heard how she did you. You can stay down here with her for a while if you like. We will give you privacy. Or we can help you load her up in the box. It travels well," I say.

"Oh! I want to have some fun with her before we leave," he says.

Draco walks over to her. The woman looks up at him and screams.

"I will dose her again," I say.

Draco smacks her across the face. "Stop that. It will be so much easier if you just cooperate," he says.

I go into the closet and retrieve another dose. Maybe I should double it. This bitch has some fight in her. I do not need her coming alive and going crazy. I damn sure do not need Tatina to hear her screaming.

I come back with the shot. I grab her arm. She begins to scream again. Draco slaps her again. I put the shot in her arm.

"It acts quickly. I will give you enough for a few days, but you will have to get your own to keep her in check. She is going to be hard to beat into submission," I say.

Draco rubs her head. "Oh, I know, but she is the one I want. She will be worth it," he says.

He checks her neck. "No one fed on your fairy. I made sure of it," I tell him.

"Just checking," he says.

Draco releases his fangs and begins tasting her. "She is perfect. Such a sweet, pure taste," he says.

"Nothing like fairy blood," I say.

"No, nothing like it. Nothing like fairy pussy either," he says.

He runs his hands over her naked body trapped in the breeding box. The box is a beautiful tool. Maybe I will make one for Tatina. Not precisely this rigid and painful. Just something to punish her when she is being a bad slave. I could make one for when she is a bad slave and one for when she is a good slave, something for fun and something for pain. She would hate it, but I would enjoy it. The thought of her naked in a box with her holes open for me to do as I please. Yes, I am going to construct one for her. I will have to drug her the first time I put her in it. I believe she would eventually submit. I am going to make her my perfect slave.

I zoned out, not paying much attention to Draco. I notice the idiots are watching him. This is not a peep show.

"Draco, we will leave you and your new bride in privacy. I will leave one idiot outside the door. If you need anything, let one of them know," I say.

He shakes his head to acknowledge what I said. He is still running his hands all over the feisty fairy. She is about to get one hell of a good time. She just does not know it.

Chapter 28

CRAIG POV

I go up to check on my precious angel sleeping. I need to check and see if she needs anything. I unlock the door to her room. I peak in, and she is still out. I think I will lay next to her in bed and hold her for a while. Maybe she needs a snack. I can make her a snack and feed it to her.

I go down to the kitchen and look in the cabinet. I take out some crackers and bread. I will cut up some cheese for her and maybe make a half of a sandwich for her. Just something to hold her over until the morning. I need her to trust me. I cannot let her starve.

I look in the refrigerator to see what I have delicious that she will not fight me over. I take out some watermelon juice. I look for a cup that she will not spill since she is so out of it. I see the breeding box bottles—the ones we use to give the breeders food and water. I grab one of those and put the watermelon juice in it. She will hate this, but if she is still out of it, then this is the only way I can get some liquid into her.

I cut her up some cheese, place the crackers and a half sandwich on the tray. Now, this is enough for now. If I can get her to eat a few bites and drink some juice, then she should be okay until morning. I cannot keep drugging her on an empty stomach.

As I walk out of the kitchen, Lila is standing in my way.

"What?" I ask her.

"Draco is having no issues from what I can hear," she says.

"Don't be a perv. Leave the man alone. He is paying big money for that breeder. Stay out of it," I say.

"Nice to see you are back to yourself. There for a minute, I thought you were going soft on me," she says.

"Mind your business bitch, and stay the hell away from Tatina. I have her right where she needs to be, and I do not need you fucking this up for me. I will have her as my perfect little slave. So back the fuck off bitch, before I strap you to a breeding box and see who will pay to fuck you," I say.

"Try me, Craig. Just fuck try me. Besides, no one is going to mess with that little fairy you have upstairs, or you for that matter. Craig, next time you threaten me, be ready. I will kill you, or better yet, I will make sure the world knows what you are," Lila says.

I push past her and go on my way. I am anxious to see my Tatina. As soon as Draco and the bitch in the basement are gone, I can carry on with my life. Maybe we will go somewhere in the mountains. Somewhere remote and away from prying eyes, someplace she can be all mine.

I unlock her door and close it behind me. I lock it from the inside. I do not want Lila disturbing my time with her. I set the bottle down on the table beside the recliner. I go to the bed. She is sleeping so sound.

I check my pocket to make sure I have a shot ready just in case I need it. I know I will need it. She may act as if she is ready to be mine, but I know she needs a lot of training. I check her phone to see if she has any messages.

Jayne has texted her, *are you okay?* I will text Jayne back for her later. There is another text on here. Unknown number *checking in on progress. Let us know* this bitch is working with the vampire authority. This fucking whore! How dare she after everything I did for her?!

It is okay. I can get her to submit and be mine. Like it or not, she is mine. Every inch of her is mine. If I have to use a breeding box every night for the rest of her life, she will be mine.

I pull the covers back. She stretches her body out. I scoop her up in my arms. "What are you doing, Craig?" she asks.

I smack her bare leg. "I told you to call me Master," I say.

I take her to the recliner and cradle her in my arms. I pick up the bottle to put it in her mouth. She spits and fights. I force it into her mouth as she struggles beneath me. I smack her bare leg again.

"Stop it. Do as I want, or it will be much worse. You need some liquid in you, and this is how we nourish breeders. So, just take it," I tell her.

I hate to think that I will have to beat her into submission. I do not want this to be a fear-based relationship, but it is heading that way. After the night we spent together, I thought this was what she wanted. But she lied. She lied to get information to turn me in. She will have to be punished for this. She is working for the authority.

She stops struggling and takes the bottle like a good girl. I watch her drink. Her eyes are watching me. She drinks the entire thing.

"I need to go to the bathroom," she says.

I pat her between the legs on the plastic diaper.

"Go ahead. I will change you when you are finished. I had to put a breeding diaper on you since you were so out of it," I say.

"I do not want to use a diaper. This is going too far," she says.

"So is lying to me. I know you are working with Glenn. You fucking whore. I will have you in a box and submitting to me. I will kill you," I say.

She looks shocked that I know. "I checked your phone," I say.

"Fuck you. You are a fucking monster," she says.

I grab her tightly. "I told you. I made it clear. You are mine. You are for me to have anyway I want. That means if I want you to dress like a whore and take it in all your holes, guess what you do. If I want you to let me baby you, guess what you do it. If I want to lock you in this room, then you deal with it. If you do not comply, guess what, breeding box," he says.

Tatina begins to cry.

"It does not have to be this way. All you have to do is be obedient," I say.

"Obedient. I was obedient, but it was not enough for you," she says.

"Tomorrow, you will be my wife. We are getting married," I tell her.

"If I say no," she asks.

"You can say no, but you are my property, so that it will do you no good. You are mine. I own you," I say.

"I thought you were a sweet man. I thought you were sorry for the things you did. You are not sorry, are you? Was it all an act?" she asks.

"You are the actress yourself. You were pretending to love me. Telling me you loved me when you did not. Are you Glenn's whore? Do you know when this is over what the authority will do with you? They will put you right back in the auction," I say.

"I meant it when I said I loved you," she says.

"You will have to prove it," I tell her.

"How?" she asks.

"By being mine, all mine in the way I want you to be," I say.

She shakes her head. That was too easy. I know she is lying to me. I cannot trust her yet. I will find a remote place to take her until she is submissive to me in every way. This is going to take some time, patients, and a lot of drugs. I will keep her dosed for now.

She curls her body into me. I continue to hold her. "I love you, master," she says.

"How I wish that were true, Tatina. I know you are lying to me. You are a lying whore," I say.

She tilts her head back and kisses my neck. "Are you hungry, Master? You can drink from me if you are," she says.

"Yes, I am, and I will drink from you because you are my blood bag. I do not need your permission to drink from you," I respond.

I cradle her tighter and lift her as I stand with her. I carry her to the bed. I lay her out gently on the bed. I push her hair back and release my fangs. I press them into her neck and begin to suckle her blood. Sweet fairy blood. It is so intoxicating.

"Master, I still need to go to the bathroom. Can I please get up and go," she asks.

I let her up to go. She comes back from the bathroom with nothing on from the waist down.

"I cleaned up so that I can be fresh for you; um, well, are you are planning to fuck me? I would like for you to fuck me, Master. I can show you how loyal I am to you," she says.

"Get on the bed, and I will take care of you," I tell her.

She lays down on the bed for me. I kiss her sweetly. I reach into my pocket and grab the shot. I stick it in her arm while she is kissing me. I cannot trust her. A few seconds later, she passes out. I sit down in the recliner and eat the cheese I brought up to feed her. Fuck her, and she can starve. I throw the sandwich in the garbage.

Chapter 29

He leaves me finally. Why in the hell did Glenn text me? I wonder what it said. I have no idea what to do or how do I feel. I feel ridiculous. He shoved a breeder bottle in my mouth and put a damn diaper on me. He plans to keep me drugged if he is treating me like a breeder. He has to make sure I have fluid and do not piss on his bed. How am going to help the woman in the basement if I am locked in here, drugged myself?

He will never trust me now. He keeps giving me this medicine that is making me feel funny. I cannot lose my focus. I have to find a way out of this. I have to find a way to get him to trust me. I think that ship has sailed. He will never trust me again.

He will be back soon to check on me. I am scared. I am confused. I am trapped. I can play along. He is planning to leave with me tonight and force me to marry him tomorrow. My only chance is to run when we leave tonight. There has to be a way to escape.

If I am really good and play along with his stupid game, then maybe I can keep him from drugging me again. I cannot move. What is he giving me? Whatever it is, it is making me paralyzed. I guess that is so I cannot run. How will I run when we leave her if I cannot move?

I am going to try to reach for my phone. It is so close. I cannot hold my eyes open. I have to reach. I have to get my phone. I need to call Jayne. I need help. Jayne, where are you? You are supposed to keep an eye on me, but here I am, all alone. Where are you?

I wake up it is late in the evening. I have been asleep a long time. He is in the recliner, and He is sitting quietly, just watching me.

"You are awake?" he says.

I try to push up in the bed. I cannot move.

"What is wrong with me?" I ask.

"I gave you more medicine so you will behave. You cannot be trusted, so this is your life until I can trust you," he says.

"You do not have to do that. I will behave, Master. I will be your good slave. I promise," I say.

"I cannot trust you, Tatina. You have lied to me too much. I know you are helping the authority," he says.

"I know I have. I will be good from now on. I promise to be loyal to you and you only," I say.

"Trust is earned, princess. You have not earned it. You have been very bad. I went through your phone. I went through everything, and you have been a very bad slave," he says.

"I will be good from now on. I promise. Please, master, give me another chance to be a good slave," I say firmly.

"There will be no phone from now on and no contact with anyone except me. Maybe if you have no phone, then you can be a good slave," he says.

What! How in the hell will I call for help. How will Jaybe find me if he gets rid of my phone?

"I understand, master. I do not deserve a phone," I say.

"I don't think you do understand. You have broken my heart, Tatina. I had not loved anyone in a long time until you. You broke me," he says.

"Come lay beside me, master. I am so cold," I say.

He keeps sitting in the recliner. I am not sure he will come to me. I need him to trust me, or I will die. I cannot live like this.

"Please, master," I beg.

"What do you think your punishment should be?" he asks.

"Punishment?" I ask.

"Yes. You will have to answer for your lies to me. You deceived me, Tatina, and you have to pay for it. So how do you think you should be punished?" he asks.

"Are you going to beat me?" I ask.

"Do you think that is appropriate? A beating? Do you think that is enough for breaking someone's heart?" he asks.

Breaking his heart, what about all the horrible things he has done. You are sick!

"I promise to behave, and I promise to be a good slave for my master," I say.

"I cannot believe you. Do you think I should sell you?" he says.

"Sell me? Are you serious?" I ask. He looks at me for a long time. "Please let me stay here with you. I want to stay with you," I say.

"We will see. It depends on how good you are to me," he says.

He gets up from the recliner. He looks so devious. I am afraid. I pull the covers over me tight. What is he going to do to me? He is going to hurt me; I can see it all over his face.

He stands next to the bed, looking at me as I cower beneath the covers. I am terrified. He pulls out another shot.

"Give me your arm," he demands.

I take my arms out from under the covers and hand it over to him. He sticks the needle in my arm and releases the medicine into me. I am never getting away. I will be with him, drugged forever. I give up.

"Good little slave, you are learning," he says.

He pulls the covers back. He looks at me up and down. He reaches under my shirt and grabs my bare breast. He pinches my nipple hard. I do not react. He runs his hand down my body and starts removing the disgusting diaper he is forcing me to wear. He grabs me between the legs hard. "You even smell like one of those breeder whores," he says.

He places his hand on my hip and rolls me onto my stomach. I can hear him removing his belt. Oh damn, He is going to beat me.

"How many times do you think you deserve to be spanked?" he asks.

"I do not know, master. I was very bad. You decide what I deserve," I answer him.

I brace myself. I know this is going to be bad. He strikes my bare bottom with his belt. It hurts, but I do not move. I have to let him have this if I ever plan to get away from him. He strikes again and again. Ten times he strikes me across my bare bottom with his leather belt.

"Good slave. You took your punishment like a good little slave," he says.

He starts rubbing where he struck me. It stings so bad. I want to cry, but I refuse to give him that. I will not give him tears.

I do not look to see what he is doing. He is quiet for a moment. I think he is removing his clothes. All of a sudden, I feel the weight of his body behind me. I have been with him before. I will just lay here and let him have me. I can do this. I can take it.

He grabs my hips and pulls them up to position me. I do not want him touching me. I can feel his hardness at the entrance of my opening. He starts rubbing himself against my bottom and then my pussy as if he is trying to decide which hole he wants to destroy. I know this is going to be bad. I just have to stay calm.

I do not move. I let him move me where he wants me. I hear something, but I do not move. I listen to him moan. He is jacking himself off over me.

"I know you do not want it. I can pleasure myself," he says.

I do not say anything. I just lay and listen. He pushes himself close to me from behind. I can feel the bed vibrate from his motions.

"Tell me you want me, slave," he demands.

I can't force myself to say it. I just lay with my bottom in the air. I am waiting for him just to take it. I know he is getting angry. He flips me over, so I have to watch him masturbate. He is between my legs, right over me, stroking himself. His face is angry as he pleasures himself.

He pushes my legs apart. He shoves himself deep inside me. I scream. I do not want him inside me. I want him to stop. I try to fight, but the medicine is making me so limp.

"Say what I want you to say. Tell me you want me, slave," he demands.

I refuse. I cannot do this. I cannot be this. He keeps pounding into me harder and harder. He leans into my neck and bites me hard, ripping my flesh. He starts sucking my neck. He is drinking from me hard. It hurts badly.

"Please stop," I scream.

This only infuriates him. He releases my neck. He slaps my face.

"No, take it. You are my slave, remember," he says.

As he rapes me, the medicine takes hold, and I begin to pass out. He smacks my face trying to keep me awake to endure the pain. I am in and out as he assaults both my holes in one and then the other.

I awake as he finishes spewing his seed all over me.

"That is your punishment. If you want to act up, you will be treated like this," he says.

I try to say I am sorry, but I cannot form the words. He covers me up. He leans down and kisses my forehead. "I will be back to punish you more later. You have a lot to make up for bitch," he says.

He leaves me in the bed, hurting and crying. I hate him. I want him to die, but there is nothing I can do.

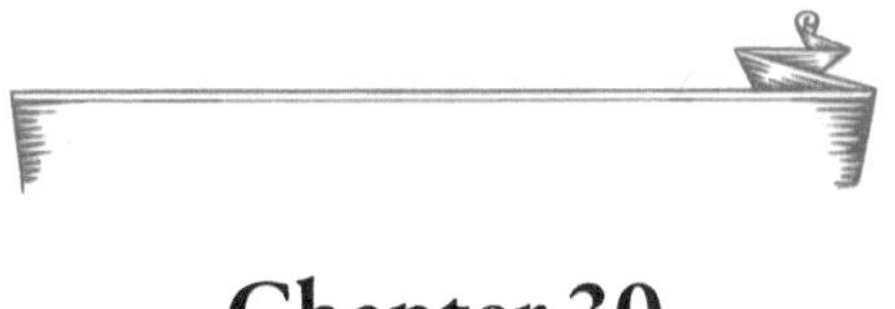

Chapter 30

JAYNE POV

I have not heard from Tatina. I am worried sick. When I try to call her phone, it goes to voicemail. I am going to the house to get her. This has to end. It will end today.

I take out my phone and call Craig, and he does not answer either. I will text him.

Hey! I am coming by to see Tatina later

I wait patiently to hear from him. After five minutes, he responds. *No visitors today. Come tomorrow*

This is not good. I call Glenn to try to get his help. No damn answer. Someone has to do something. We have put her in danger, and no one cares that she could die. The authority set her up.

Glenn finally texts me back. * We are going in tonight to get her. Stay put*

They better get her out of that house before something terrible happens. I have a horrible feeling about this. I do not trust Glenn or anyone. I have to get her. I will do it myself.

I cannot take it. I am going to get her with or without the help of the authority. This is on me. I put her in danger. I thought this would be a good thing for her and him. I was so wrong. I was so wrong.

I gather my purse and keys. I lock up my house and run down to my car. Glenn is standing by my car. He knows I am not willing to wait.

"Where are you going?" he asks, hissing his words.

"I am going to go get her," I answer.

"I figured as much. Just give me an hour to gather some people to go in to get her. Just an hour, Jayne. Give me one fucking hour before you do something stupid," he says.

"You have one hour. I will be close by waiting to take her," I say.

Glenn shakes his head and leaves quickly. I get into my car. I need somewhere to wait for one hour. I will give him one hour to get her, and then I go in myself and kill that bastard.

I drive to a bar and park. That looks like Lila's car. I grab my phone and my purse and quickly exit the car. I am going to have a few words with this woman and maybe beat her ass.

I go into the bar and look around for her. I finally see her sitting at a table in the back. I walk over to her and glare down at the bitch.

"Can I sit?" I ask. I do not wait for an answer. I sit down.

"Sure. I guess since we are old friends," she says.

"We are not friends, and you know why I am here," I ask her.

"Yes, you cannot get a hold of your sweet little friend," she says.

"Yes. I am worried about her," I say.

"She is fine. Probably planning her wedding," she says.

"Wedding. What damn wedding?" I ask.

"Craig is marrying her tomorrow. They will live happily ever after," she says. Her face says torment and pain.

"What? I have been trying to call her. She will not talk to me," I say.

"Yeah. Well, they are all over one another. I cannot get a word in with him about the business. He is only worried about her and her needs," Lila says.

"So she is okay," I ask.

"Yep. She is just perfect," she responds.

I know she is lying. Tatina would not marry him not unless he were forcing her to marry him. I know what he is doing to her. He is torturing her for her light or worse.

"Listen, Jayne, as much as I would love to sit here and talk to you about your sweet little friend, I am meeting someone. So could you carry on somewhere else?" she demands.

"Sure, sorry to intrude on you. I just wanted to know if she is okay since Craig told me not to come to the house," I say.

"Well, he has company right now," she slips.

"Company?" I inquire.

"None of your concern. Just come by tomorrow. I will make sure she is waiting on you. The two of you can talk about her perfect little wedding," she says.

I get up from her table and walk to an empty one far enough away from her. I can still see who she is meeting but not look conspicuous. I sit waiting for the hour to pass. I see a handsome young vampire come into the bar as I am waiting. Draco. I know that vampire from anywhere. He is banned from authority auctions, and here he is buying from Craig. Hmm. This makes sense. Draco has money to burn, and Craig has breeders.

Draco is Craig's company; I just know it. The two of them are all cozied up talking. I wish I could hear what they are saying. Why wasn't I born with that gift?

I bet Draco is Craig's biggest buyer. He cannot buy from the Vampire Authority auctions. He has to go elsewhere. He is a brutal, vile excuse for a vampire. I hope he doesn't get his hands on Tatina. He must be here for whoever is at the house. The difficult sale belongs to Draco. It had to be Draco, and I should have known.

I cannot wait any longer. I have to go get her. I get up from the table. I lay money on the table to cover my drink and turn to leave.

"Leaving so soon," I hear from behind me.

I turn to see Draco.

"Yes, I have an appointment," I say.

"Really, I thought you might be trying to get information about that girl. You know your friend," he says.

"You are not going to help me, Draco. So do not even pretend you are going to help me," I say.

I push past him.

"I can help you. It will cost you, but I can help. Do you want my help, or do you want her to suffer? You have no idea what he is doing to her and what he plans for her," he says.

I stop. I turn back to him. "How can you help, and why would you help me?" I ask.

"I know things. I know she is miserable. I know he is torturing her. He is trying to get her to submit to him. She is very reluctant about his lifestyle. Much like your precious Julie was reluctant to him. That did not turn out very well for her, now did it?" he says.

"Leave my sister out of this. She was sick in the head and lost her mind," I demand.

He moves in closer to me. "How could you send that sweet little fairy in there knowing what would happen to her?" he asks.

"I did not know," I answer.

"Oh yes, you did. Admit it, you knew. Everything that is happening to her is all your fault. Now do you want my help or not?" he says.

He stands before. He wants me to want his help. He is an arrogant little jerk.

"Glenn cannot help you with this. You know that, don't you? I am the only one that can. You know Glenn set her up and is using her. He is not going to rescue her. Glenn will leave her in there to die," he says.

"If I let you help me, then what? What do you want?" I ask.

Draco moves closer, putting his arm around me. "I want to leave the house with my prize. I want to be able to bid at auctions again. I want you to let me take you on a date and see what you taste like when you are all wet," he says.

I pull away from him. "I cannot do any of those things. I do not have the authority to reinstate your bidding privileges, and you disgust me," I say.

"Well, my little fairy friend. She will have a horrible life as his sex slave, breeding machine, and subservient wife. Is that what you want for her? Did you and Glenn not send her in there to steal my prize?" he asks.

He pulls me back close to him. I begin shaking. He brushes my bangs away from my face. He gets close to my lips. "You can do it. Let me have my three little demands, and I will bring her to you. She will be in perfect condition and ready to leave with you. I will not touch her, I promise. You, on the other hand, yeah, I want to touch you," he says.

I shake my head yes. I do not know how in the hell I can get him back on the auction list, but I have to do it for her.

"Seal our deal with a kiss," he says and leans in to kiss me.

"I am not going to kiss the devil," I say. I pull away from him.

He grabs me and presses his lips to mine.

"You pig," I say.

"I may be a pig, but this pig is going to save your friend. I will bring her to your house. Give me an hour," he says.

I shake my head and run out of the bar. I cannot believe I am trusting that demon to help me, but what choice do I have. Draco could kill Craig easily. I don't care what he does as long as he gets Tatina out of there.

Chapter 31

DRACO POV

Man, she is one hot little fairy, and now she has to let me take her on a date. I will show her a good time. Maybe charm her right out of her corporate pants. Yummy.

"What was that about?" Lila asks.

I turn to see the little minion of Craig behind me being nosey as usual. Why does Craig keep her around? She is such a cunt.

"I do not think it concerns you, Lila," I say, hissing at her, so she knows I am pissed off at her.

"Sorry, Draco. I should not be in your business," she says.

Nosey little bitch. She needs to mind her business.

"Just do what I asked. Get my purchase out of the house now. I want her loaded and on her way to my house within the hour. No exceptions and no fuck ups," I tell her.

"I will get the guys on it. It might take longer than an hour," she says.

This infuriates me. Lila is the most incompetent person I have ever met in my life.

"Why? Pick up the box, throw it in the van and start driving. I want her to be there when I get there. I expect you to make the ride with her personally. Got it!" I demand.

"Yes, sir. I will take care of it personally as you request," she says.

Now I have to wait. Just wait on my purchase to be loaded up, and then I will go get Tatina. Then I can have my way with little miss Jayne. Jayne is the perfect prize.

I watch Lila leave. She is headed to the house to get my purchase loaded up and on her way. I have a hard time believing Lila can be obedient or competent, but I guess that is why Craig keeps her around. She is obedient when she wants to be. Maybe I will keep her with me after I take Tatina. Lila should be with me. She needs to see what it is like to be in a box.

I walk out to my car. I will give them a few minutes and then I will go to the house. I know they are planning to raid the house today. I need to be quick. As long as my purchase is out, I do not really care. I would like to help Jayne just to get my auction privileges back, but I will not risk being caught up in all of this. I guess I am caught up in it. I need to make sure Tatina does not know I am involved in any way.

I get in my car and start it. I check the time. I will wait five more minutes. I look behind me and see Glenn. Shit. I have got to get this party started. I cannot wait any longer. I put the car in drive and leave.

I will take the back way; it is quicker. There should not be any traffic right now. I need to hurry up and get to the house before the vampire authority raids it. They better get my little purchase out before the raid. My purchase does not need to end up in the authority auction, and I do not need any trouble from the authority today.

I take the back roads speeding to get to the house before Craig runs with Tatina. He thinks he is slick. He forgets some of us can read minds. He is planning to run. He needed my money to run. Too bad for him. He is not getting it.

I pull into the drive of the house. I push my code to get into the gate. The gate opens, and I drive up to the house. No one is outside. Good. Lila is occupied. The van is gone, so she and those idiots that work for Craig are on their way with my purchase to my house.

Step one, complete my purchase, is gone, and the minions are away— time for Draco to play. I open the door. No one is around. I listen for Craig. I hear nothing but singing. I follow the sound of the singing to an upstairs bedroom.

I try to open the door gently.

"Who is it?" I hear Craig call from the other side.

I push the door open. Damn. You sick bastard. I know I am a perverse piece of shit, but this goes beyond that.

"We need to talk?" I say.

He is singing to that fairy in a recliner with a bottle shoved down her throat. She struggles, and he smacks her leg.

"Stop it bitch," he says to her.

I thought he was in love with her. This is not love. This is something unnatural.

"What do you want, Draco? The idiots have already left with your fairy. I assume you paid Lila," he says.

I walk closer to him, and this disgusting scene playing out in front of me. I cannot believe what I am seeing. I have seen some bad shit in my time with these auctions, but this takes the cake.

"I know, but there is something we need to discuss," I say, inching closer.

"Draco, as soon as I finish feeding this little bitch I am leaving. No more auctions for me. I am going to focus on her and our family. I love her," he says.

I step close to him. I can see the light in Tatina's eyes. She is begging for my help. She needs out of this.

"I see. But we still have something to discuss before I leave," I say.

Tatina struggles to push the bottle out of her mouth. Craig smacks her again. Her legs are covered in bruises. Dried blood and feces are running down her leg. She smells like urine.

"What is it?" he demands.

"Her. I want her," I say, inching closer to her.

"You cannot have her. She is mine. She is all mine. She is not for sale," he says.

"The vampire authority is on its way here to raid you. They are going to take her anyway. Let me pay you for her. You can get away clean. I will take her, and she will make me very happy," I say.

"No, we are leaving. You cannot have her. I will kill her before I let anyone take her," he says.

Craig tries to stand with her in his arms. I push him back into the recliner. I put my hand firmly around his neck. "You do not really have an option here. Give her to me," I say.

Craig releases his fangs and snarls at me.

"You are no match for me. I am much stronger than you. Take the money and go. This is your last chance to give her to me," I say.

He holds on to Tatina tightly. "She is mine. She is all mine," he demands.

I tighten my grip around his neck. I pick him up out of the recliner by his neck. He drops Tatina to the floor. She moans as she hits the floor. I slam Craig against the wall. He is snarling and fighting me. He cannot break free from me. I hold him in place. I look back to see if Tatina is okay. She is not moving. I snap Craig's neck quickly. I leave him lying for the vampire authority to find. They can deal with him.

I rush over to Tatina. She is breathing. I grab a blanket from the bed. I wrap her up tightly in the blanket. We have got to get out of here before the vampire authority gets here. I have a feeling they want her for something terrible.

I cradle her in my arms. Sorry, love, no time to clean you up. We will take care of that later. I carry her down the stairs and out the front door. Still no sign of anyone. Not even the vampire authority.

I place Tatina in my car. I buckle her in. I wonder how much of those drugs he gave her. She is completely in another world. She is limp and drooling. I hope she makes it. Please do not die on me. Jayne will kill me.

I get in the car and begin to drive away from the house. As we exit the drive, I see the vampire authority is coming. Shit. I cannot go that way. I turn to head to the interstate. Sorry, Jayne looks like Tatina is going with me. Jayne will have to do a pick up.

"Am I okay?" she mumbles.

"Yes, just rest. You are somewhat safe now," I say.

She closes her eyes and drifts back off into sleep. I look behind me, and we are not being followed. I turn off on the interstate. It looks like I gained a houseguest for a while.

Chapter 32

DRACO POV

I pull into my drive. There is no van and no minions. Either they have been and gone, or Glenn got them. I have not received a text from anyone. Not even Jayne. I am worried about Jayne and my purchase.

I get out of the car and go around to help Tatina. I open the door and scoop her up. She is still so weak. I take her into my home carefully. I take her directly to the guest room. I lay her on the bed, still wrapped in the blanket. I enter the guest bathroom and begin running a hot bath for her. I have got to clean her up. I cannot believe the shape she is in right now. How could anyone do this to someone? It makes me sick.

I leave the water running and go to retrieve her. I undress her very quickly. She is covered in bruises. I remove the diapers. What has he done to her? There is not a part of her body that is not covered in bruises or blood. There are marks from a belt all over her. This makes me think of Deanne and Emma. The site of Tatina is breaking my heart. If I still had one. It has been a long time since I really felt anything for anyone.

I carry her to the tub. I place her in the water. She jerks as I lay her in the water. I keep my arm behind her head. She is still out of it. I wash her body carefully. The dried blood and feces that coat her body is vanishing into the water. No worries, love, I will take care of you.

I unplug the tub to release it and refill it with clean water. I wash her again and again, trying to make her clean. She opens her eyes.

"Where am I?" she asks.

"You are my guest. I could not have you smelling up the place. I am sorry if I scared you," I say.

She nods and closes her eyes. She drifts back off into slumber. I pick her up out of the tub. I grab a towel and wrap it around her. I carry her back to the guest bed. I lay her on the bed wrapped in the towel. I am sure I have something here to fit you. At one time, I kept things just to help the women of the Auctions, back when I could help several at a time. Now it is just one at a time.

I reach into a drawer and find a shirt and a pair of shorts. I slip the shirt over her head. She doesn't move. I touch her leg to put the shorts on her.

"Please don't. I can't take anymore. I am sorry. Do not rape me again," she cries.

I sip them up quickly and cover her with a sheet. I take her old clothes and the blanket out of the room. I take the disgusting things to the trash. As I am about to return to her, I hear moving in the basement. I go down to check on the woman.

Lila left her in the box. I unfasten the belts and chains. I release her. "Are you okay?" I ask.

"No, I am not," she says.

"I will have some food brought down for you," I say.

"Are you going to rape me now?" she asks.

"No. I have no intentions of harming you, not today or ever. I plan to help you, but you made it really hard," I say.

"Thank you. I am sorry. I was afraid. They were horrible at that place. That hurt me a lot," she says.

I leave her in the basement and return to the upstairs. I go into the kitchen to let the cook know we have guests.

"Henry, please prepare a meal for the guest downstairs and one in the guest room, please," I say.

He acknowledges my request and continues with what he is doing. I leave the kitchen to check on Tatina.

My phone is buzzing in my pocket. I take it out to look to see who it is. It is Jayne.

is she okay?

I reply *she will be*

I go back up the stairs to the guest room to check on my guest. She is still sleeping. I know when she wakes, all of this won't be very clear for her. I have to handle my little purchase in the basement at some point. Right now, I need to focus on Tatina.

I sit down on the end of the bed. I watch her sleep. Why in the hell was he punishing her so hard? What could she have done to make him lose it like this? I have heard stories about things he has done. I am no saint, but this is horrible. I cannot believe what I am seeing.

The door opens slightly. It is Henry.

"I took the little lady in the basement food and a coke. She was most grateful. Here is something for her if she is awake," he says.

"Thank you, Henry," I say.

I gently shake Tatina. "Tatina, you need to wake and eat," I say.

She gently rubs her eyes. She looks at me. "Where am I?" she asks.

"Jayne asked me to take you from Craig, so I did. Do you remember anything?" I ask her.

"No, I am so fuzzy. My head feels icky," she says.

"You need to eat. We need to get those drugs out of your system," I say.

"Can you help me up, please?" she asks.

I lean over and pick her up. She is so light. I walk over to her food and sit her down. She groans. She begins to eat slowly.

"You are okay. I am going to let Jayne know where you are and that you are up and moving," I say.

She tries to smile, but her face is swollen. He beat her face. Is there anywhere he did not touch her?

"Thank you. I thought I was going to die there or worse, live," she says.

"What did he do to you?" I ask.

"He was mad. He found a message from Glenn on my phone. He knew I was helping them," she says.

"Glenn is no saint. Do not be fooled. The authority is very corrupt. They wanted something, but I am not sure what," I say.

"He was treating me like a breeder. Glenn told me to start calling him master and that it would trigger something in him to make him trust me. Glenn said it was what Julie called him," She says.

"Well, Glenn set you up. I am sorry to say. It set in motion a very volatile game. Craig is a son of a bitch, and he took a lot of anger out on you," I say.

"I just wanted to help. Glenn said there were women in the basement being mistreated, and he needed my help. I only wanted to help," she says.

"Tatina, the woman is here. She is in my basement, but she is not hurt. I am going to help her. I promise you no harm will come to her or you," I say.

"Why are you buying women to breed?" she asks.

"It is not what you think. I will explain everything to you when you feel better. Please eat. I am going to call Jayne for you," I say.

She continues eating. I pull out my phone to call Jayne. There is a text.

Trust no one. I am on the run. Give Tatina my love. Would you please keep her safe

Oh shit. What have I gotten myself into now?

"Tatina, you are going to be my guest for a while. Jayne is in trouble," I say.

I show her my phone. She begins to sob. "I cannot lose Jayne. Everything in my life has gone straight to hell," Tatina sobs. Do not worry, I will take care of you, Tatina.

Chapter 33

TATINA POV

My entire body hurts. I am so weak from the drugs. Here I am, a guest in a vampire's home. He is being kind, but I cannot forget he also has someone in his basement. I cannot wait to hear the explanation for all of this. Maybe things are not how they seem, and nothing ever is anymore.

Poor Jayne. She tried to help me and look where it landed her on the run. I bet it was Glenn. Why did Glenn pretend to help me or tell me to do those things only to text me and set off my own personal hell? It is Glenn's fault this happened to me. Well, most of it.

The things he did to me. The way he hit me. The way he raped me repeatedly. I soiled myself over and over. The smell of my bodily fluids all over me while he was pounding into me. Then beat me for not enjoying it. I hate him.

Those stories of how he loved his precious Julie. Lies, it was all just all Lies. I hope he is dead. I hope he can never hurt another woman again. I wonder if any of it was true. I hope someone kills Glenn too. They all deserve to die for what they have done. I am so angry at the authority!

I ate everything Draco provided me. I wonder why he is being nice. What does he stand to gain for helping me? Why would Jayne trust him to care for me? These people and this auction business have to stop. The fairies have to be protected. The hybrids need someone to protect them.

I am just a nobody; how can I think I could ever protect anyone. I am not anyone important. I am just a young woman in the absolute worst mess. At least I am not in the basement.

"Do you need help back to the bed?" Draco asks me.

He has sat there silently. "I am still very weak. My body hurts, and I feel dizzy. If you do not mind helping me," I say.

"I will be gentle, I promise," he says.

He scoops me up easily. He carries me back to the bed. He lays me across it. "I will send someone to get you clothes. If there is anything else you need, let me or Henry know," he says.

"Thank you. I would very much appreciate everything you are doing for me. I do not understand why, but that you," I say.

"There are a few things that belonged to my sister in the drawers. You are welcome to any of it. She was tiny like you," he says.

"Was?" I inquire.

"Yes, was tiny. She died a few years ago. That is a story for another day. I do not think I want to open that box up right now," he says.

"Was she a vampire too," I ask?

"No, she was a fairy, just like you. She was a headstrong hybrid and a badass, also like you," he says.

"There is nothing badass about me," I say.

"You have a gift, and someday you will tap into it and scare the shit out of all of them. I hope I get to see it," Draco says.

He turns to leave me to rest.

"Wait," I say.

He stops. "Are you a hybrid?" I ask.

I can tell he is not ready to talk to me about all of this.

"Tatina, I am the bad guy. You need to trust me long enough to be safe and then get far away. There is no need to get to know me. Let me help you and then go on about your life," he says.

"Please tell me, are you?" I ask again.

"Yes, I am a hybrid. More vampire than fairy but a hybrid nonetheless," he answers reluctantly.

"Did they take her?" I ask.

"Who?" he says.

"Your sister. Did the vampire authority take her from you?" I ask.

"Tatina, please, not right now. I really need to go down and settle in my other house guest," he says.

"Please do not hurt her," I say.

"I have no intentions of hurting her. I never have any intentions of hurting anyone. I have done nothing but help these poor women escape," Draco says.

"I am so confused," I say.

"I know, and I will be happy to explain everything later. I need to go check on her and make sure she is comfortable and has everything she needs," he says.

He leaves the room. I am more confused right now than the day I was dragged out of my home and painted up like a whore to be auctioned off to the highest bidder. What are these people really doing?

I want to know everything that is going on. First, I have to heal, and my body is a mess. I am weak. I am so sleepy. I lay my head down and drift off into a perfect slumber.

I awake to the smell of the most delicious food. Henry has brought in three trays. I hear Draco coming up the stairs. He is talking with someone. He opens the door. A beautiful young woman enters with him.

"Tatina, this is Aurora," he says.

She runs into the room and lands on the bed with me.

"Careful," Draco says.

She wraps her arms around me. "Are you okay?" she asks me.

"I am now. Are you?" I ask.

"I am now. Draco saved me," she says.

"Me too," I say.

This man has a lot of explaining to do. The meanest man on the planet is out saving fairies, and no one knows it. He is the badass hybrid, not me.

"Let me help you so we can all eat together. I am starving," she says.

She gently takes my hand. I am still so weak. Draco rushes over to scoop me up yet again. I have to start walking again soon.

"Will the drugs ever be out of my system?" I ask.

"I have no idea how much he was giving you. Maybe by tomorrow, you can walk. Aurora can help you bathe until you are steady. I am sure me doing it was embarrassing enough," Draco says.

"That would be great," I say.

"I am having a bed moved up here in this room so the two of you can share a room," he says.

"Oh. So you do not keep people tied up in the basement," I ask.

"No, I had to have her delivered like that. I tried talking to her at Craig's she wouldn't listen to me. She forced me into putting on a show," Draco says.

"I am so thankful. You have to know I was terrified there. Lila was awful. She kept taking my clothes and beating me. That creepy guy, enmo or mon, whatever his name was, kept licking my face. It was gross," Aurora says.

"Why did you finally trust him?" I ask.

"He drank from me, and we connected thoughts. He let me know he was trying to help. I was still scared. I was so scared he was going to rape me when he got me here. Even after I saw how pure his thoughts were. Lila kept telling me all the way here about the awful things he would do to me. I believed her; that bitch is crazy as hell," she says.

"You are both safe now, and Jayne owes me dinner?" Draco says jokingly.

"What?" I ask.

"I approached Jayne to get you out. Lila was planning to kill you. When I found out, I approached Jayne. She does not know I bid on these women to help them. I told her I would help as long as she didn't interfere with my purchase, restored my auction privileges, and had dinner with me. I have to be careful of my thoughts. Some of you can read minds. I do not want what I do to get out. I have been doing this for a long time. I got in a lot of trouble once and lost the people who helped me. Now it is just me, and I have to keep the lie up. I have to live as an evil vampire," Draco says.

"I see. This facade must be draining on you. You have no friends and live a life all alone. It must be hard," I say.

"It is all worth it," he says.

"You don't care that people think you are worse than the devil," I ask?

"No. I have something I have to do. It means I have to be what they need me to be. The only people that know are the fairies I have helped. I want to keep it that way," he says.

I nod in acknowledgment of his good deeds. "I understand," I say.

"I am going to leave the two of you to talk. I have to try to find Jayne. I will let you know what I find out," Draco says.

We open the third tray left untouched to find cheesecake. Aurora and I devour the cheesecake. I have not had something so yummy in ages. I am so thankful for Draco.

Chapter 34

DRACO POV

There is only one person who can help Jayne. I hate to even go down that road. It is a risk I will have to take. Tatina needs Jayne. I can keep her and Aurora safe for now, but they cannot stay here forever. I have to help Aurora move on and Tatina too.

I pull my phone out of my pocket, and I scroll down to find the name Sin. I hit the contact name to send a text.

Urgent. Jayne is missing. Please help

It will be a long wait, but if anyone can find her, Sin can. She is good at her job. Her job is finding people who do not want to be found. I hope I am never on her bad side. Well, I was at one time, but not anymore.

I pull out my laptop while I wait for Sin to text me back. I check the underground auction sites to see if Lila is going to continue to operate under Craig's name. I select the favorite tab and click on the site. The site is blacked out. Good. At least that is a comfort, another site taken down for now if Craig is out of business that gives me a little breathing room, at least for a day or two.

I will never kill all the sites or rescue all the fairies, but I have done my part. Let them think I am evil. I do not care. The viler they believe I am, the more the underbelly of our society will trust me. The auctions have to be stopped. Glenn cannot be trusted to do it. I wonder if he is in on it.

I cannot believe he told Tatina to walk into that game with Craig. He knew it would trigger him after what happened with Julie. He knew what would happen to her and how he would react. He was willing to play with her life. I will make sure to tell Sin all about it. Maybe Sin can pay a visit to Glenn.

I hear the women giggling. It is nice to listen to them. I am happy for them. If nothing else, they have each other for now. Jayne would probably agree to help Aurora. I am sure she would rather take her than let her stay here with me. After all, she thinks I am going to breed her. Never. I would never put a woman through what happened to my sister. To hell with the vampire authority and all of their bullshit. It is time for this to end all of this.

I hear running. I turn to see the two of them laughing and running into the kitchen. They are both all smiles and happy.

"You guys hungry," I ask.

"Yes, look, I am moving around all by myself," Tatina says.

"Must've been something magic in the cheesecake," I say.

"Must've been. My body started healing after I ate it," she says.

"Yeah, fresh vampire blood will do that to you. I was afraid to use it when you first got here. You were too bad," I say.

She runs to me and hugs me. "Thank you for saving me. I will owe you my life forever," she says.

"It was my pleasure," I say.

"Can we go outside and walk around?" Aurora asks.

"Not yet. You are not a prisoner here, but we have to be careful for a while. I cannot let anyone know that Tatina is here or that you are not breeding in the basement. I have to keep up my shady evil facade," I say.

"We understand. We both appreciate you," Aurora says. Tatina nods in agreement.

"Listen, I know you feel like a new woman, but it will wear off. The vampire blood does heal, but that energy burst will fade. Take it easy for a few days. You do not need to injury yourself," I tell her.

"Can we explore the house, or is that off-limits?" Tatina asks.

"Yes. Again you are not a prisoner. Feel free to roam. If anyone comes, I will get to you quickly. You are safe with me," I say.

They are so full of energy. Oh, to be in my 20's again. They scurry off to explore the house. There is not really anything for them to see. It is just a house.

I hear my phone ding. I check it. It is Sin.

I am on it. Jayne is one of the good ones. I will find her for you. Give me a day

That is taken care of. Sin will find her and bring her back safely. If Jayne needs help, I will help her. If I helped her, I would have to tell her my secret. I am not sure I am ready for that. Too many people know already, but Jayne, I think I could trust Jayne.

"I am leaving, sir," Henry says.

I forgot he was still here. He has been with me for so long. He has worked for me since I pulled his daughter out of an auction in Mexico. He should've retired a long time ago. I think he would keep coming if I fired him. He owes me nothing but feels like he owes me everything.

His daughter is now living a new life with a new identity. I wish I could say that about Deanne, but her downfall was my fault. I sent her to the work wolf camp to gather information, and shit went wrong. I blame myself for her death every day.

Aurora and Tatina are running around the house like kids. I hear them giggling. The laughter in the house is a pleasant tone. Once a long time ago, I lived in a house that was happy. There was a time when so many were helped, and that gave me a purpose, but after the raid, everything became hard. Angela and Aspen went off the grid, and Tia, my sweet friend, changed her name and does not speak to me anymore unless there is a problem that needs to be fixed. She is no longer Tia and never will be again. Now, she is a warrior for the cause.

"You know it is okay to be happy for a moment. You did a good thing for them," Henry says.

"I am not sure I know how to be happy, Henry. I will see you in the morning," I tell Henry.

He leaves. My phone begins to buzz. I grab it; there is no way she found Jayne this fast.

I found her

Sin, Hell yes. She found her.

Bring her to me as quickly as you can I text back.

I found her. I do not have her. But I will get her for you

She texts back.

I know she will. I don't know how but she always comes through. She can do things other cannot, but at what cost. I often wonder how she is doing. We were friends so long ago and then she became this person.

I try to occupy myself while I wait. It may not be today. It may be a few days before she has her. I am not going to say anything to Tatina yet. I would hate for her to worry more about what is going on. Not right now when she is enjoying herself. They both deserve to have a nice quiet night.

I sit in the kitchen, enjoying only the sounds of them talking. The house is quiet. My sister always enjoyed quiet nights. The quiet never lasts. After the quiet, the sadness creeps in and haunts me.

Tatina comes running into the kitchen.

"There is something wrong with Aurora," she says.

I speed past Tatina to find Aurora lying on the floor.

"What happened?" I ask.

"I do not know. She just fainted," Tatina says.

I touch her forehead. She is very hot. I pick her up and carry her up the stairs.

"Tatina, come with us. I want you to stay with her at all times," I say.

I hope this is not what I think it is. I push open the door to Tatina's room. I lay Aurora on the bed. She blinks rapidly.

"What is wrong with her?" Tatina asks.

I do not answer her. Aurora opens her eyes slightly. I need her to wake up. I have questions I need answers to so I can make the right decision about how to treat her.

"Aurora, I need you to listen to me. I need you to tell me if anything happened at Craig's," I say very softly to her.

Aurora shakes her head yes. "Was it a vampire who did it to you or a human?" I ask her.

"It was the wolf," she says.

"A wolf, are you sure? Who was the wolf?" I ask her.

"Emno, the wolf," she says.

"What is going on?" Tatina asks. She is panicking.

I sit Tatina down. "Listen to me very carefully. She is going to have a dreadful night. She could die, but we are going to try very hard to save her. She is pregnant by a wolf," I say.

"What?" Tatina says, obviously confused.

"Hybrids cannot mate with wolves," I tell her.

"What will happen to her?" she asks.

"If she survives the fever, then she will live. I need you to help me keep her cool all night. We can wet blankets with cold water. It is not going to be pleasant, but we have to try. I am going to get some ice so we can pack her in ice in the tub," I say.

Tatina sits with her new friends while I retrieve the ice. I return quickly and start filling the tub with ice. I pick Aurora up and put her in the tub. Tatina wets blankets with cold water. We wrap Aurora up tightly in the blankets.

"How did you know what is happening to her?" Tatina asks.

"This is how my sister died. A wolf raped her. She was in an auction, and this is what killed her. A damn wolf killed her," I tell her.

Tatina sits down beside the tub. "I won't leave her. I promise," she says.

"I know you will take care of her. I will be back," I say. I leave Tatina to bring up more ice. Aurora probably will not make it, but I want to try to save her. She deserves the chance to live.

Chapter 35

TATINA POV

I lay on the floor beside the tub, watching Aurora suffer. I cannot believe what I am watching. For a brief moment, I felt happiness. Now I lay here on the floor watching my new friend covered in ice and blankets, trying to cool her fever.

I don't have a complete understanding of what has happened. Draco did not explain much, only that she was pregnant by a wolf and very sick. His sister died this way. How hard must it have been for him to watch his sister die like this? No wonder he is such a hard ass.

Aurora whimpers. I reach for her. She cannot die. I need something good in my life. That is selfish of me. I want her to live. I want to see her make a life beyond the horror she and I have experienced. She deserves to live.

"You to have to survive the night, please. I need you," I say to her.

I take her hand and hold it. I cannot lose her. What if I lose her and Jayne? I have to have faith in Draco. I am putting all my trust in him that he will save the two of them. I do not even know him, but I know he is good.

Aurora continues to shift her body under the ice. I wonder what happens if she survives the night. Draco said if she survives the fever, she will live. What about the child inside her? Will the baby survive? Then what will happen to the baby? Has a hybrid ever survived something like this?

Draco returns to us. He peers into the bathroom but doesn't speak. He was right about one thing I am starting to feel weak again. I have to hold myself together for Aurora.

"How long will it take for her fever to go down," I ask Draco.

He shifts, not answering me immediately. His mind is spinning, I can tell. Maybe he doesn't want to respond to me. Perhaps he wants me just to be quiet and wait.

"Tatina, If she breaks the fever, she will be okay, but there are only a very few that have ever survived breeding with a wolf. A hybrid is not made for wolf breeding. Prepare yourself. This may not end well," he says.

I turn back to Aurora. I watch her take in a shallow breath. Oh, Aurora, you got to make it. I will be there for you.

"What would happen to her baby?" I ask.

"That is complicated, but we will figure it out," he says.

"Tatina," Aurora whimpers my name.

"I am here. Please rest," I say.

"I am so hot," she says meekly.

"SShhh," I rub her hand.

I hear Draco's phone buzzing in his pocket. He takes it out and looks at it.

"Sin has Jayne," he says.

Thank goodness. At least something is going right.

"When will she be here," I ask.

Draco steps into the bathroom and kneels on the floor. He looks at precious Aurora fighting for her life and then looks back at me.

"Tatina, I sent a very special person to retrieve her. I know she has her, but I do not know her condition. We will not know until Sin brings her here. So until then, we will focus on our friend making it through the night," he says.

"What will happen to us all?" I ask.

"We will figure it out?" he says.

"Draco, are you going to continue trying to stop them?" I ask.

"Until the day I die, Tatina and you know us vampires live a long time," he says.

I lay my head on the side of the tub and listen to Aurora breathe. Whenever I hear her inhale, I know we are one step closer to making it through the night. "You can do this, Aurora," I say to her.

I hear a commotion downstairs. "Stay here. Lock the door," Draco says.

He rushes out of the bathroom to investigate the disturbance. I quickly lock the door. I wish I had supernatural abilities of some kind so I could protect us. One if for damn sure, when this is over, someone is helping me figure out how to tap into my powers.

I listen but hear nothing. The commotion stops. It is way too quiet. I hope Draco is okay. Who am I kidding? He is very strong. I suddenly hear footsteps approaching. I dare not move. I press my ear to the door listening.

"Tatina," I hear from the other side of the door.

I open the door to see Draco standing in front of me.

"Sin is here. She brought Jayne. Jayne is dead. I am so sorry, Tatina," Draco says as he pulls me into his arms.

"Can I see her? What happened? Who killed her?" I ask. I sob into his chest.

"Sin found her in a hotel outside of New Orleans hiding from the authority. She was already dead when she went in to bring her here. I am sure it was the authority that killed her. Jayne knew too much, and I am sure they needed to get rid of her," he says.

"I want to see her," I say.

Draco releases me from his embrace. "No, you do not. We will give her a funeral tomorrow. We have to focus on Aurora tonight," he says.

He is right; I need to help Aurora through the night. Tomorrow I have to bury my friend. I sit back on the floor beside Aurora. I cannot cry. I cannot be upset right now. I need to keep my focus on Aurora.

Draco sits with me on the floor. We continue to watch Aurora. Draco repacks the ice on her body and checks to see if she still has a fever.

"I think her fever is coming down," he says.

"What will happen after her fever breaks?" I ask.

"She will be unwell for a few weeks, and her baby will have a slim chance of survival," he says.

"Are you going to make us leave?" I ask.

Draco reaches for me to comfort me. "You are Aurora are welcome here for as long as you need me," he says.

"I think the three of us need each other," I say.

I lay my head back on the side of the tub and drift off into a deep slumber. I dream of fairies. I dream of hearts and flowers. I dream of a peaceful meadow where we are free.

I awake. The sun is shining through the window in the bathroom. Aurora is cold. I give her a nudge to wake her. She does not move. They will pay for this.

I step out of the bathroom, looking for Draco.

"She's dead," I sob.

I run for him. I melt into him. He holds me like a father comforting a daughter. "I have no one now," I say.

"You have me for as long as you need me. I will protect you for always," he says.

"I have to make them pay. Please teach me to be a hybrid. Teach me to be a badass that you say I am so I can stop the auctions," I sob.

"I will teach you everything about being a hybrid. You can help me stop them. It will not be easy, but I know you can do it, Tatina. You are a badass just like my sister," he says.

We buried Jayne and Aurora at sunset. He allowed me time to grieve. When I was ready, he showed me how to bid on breeders. He taught me how to act and what to say. He taught me to mind my thoughts and be ruthless in the presence of others. With my new identity and will to succeed, I helped Draco rescue thousands of breeding fairies from all other the world. We have not stopped them all, but we have saved many.

Chapter 36

Draco POV

Tatina has struggled so much over the last few years with everything that happened to her while she was with Craig. She has never went into much details about those nights she was with him before I could rescue her. She has consumed herself in her work.

She works day and night trying to find auctions to shut the shit show down. I work by her side mostly. I did not go with her a few months ago. She went into a auctioneers house. What she found pushed her to work harder. She pulled three women out. Only one survived, and she was left permanently blind. After that day Tatina has worked harder than ever to stop the auctions.

I think our greatest victory came when the vampire authority outlawed auctions. Underground auctions, which have always been illegal now carry the death penalty. Anyone found operating an underground auction will be burned to death.

I sit this morning waiting for her to come back from her hunt last night. She wanted to go alone. I let her go by herself when she wants. She is tough. I have no doubt she can take care of herself.

I fell head over heels in love with her a few months after she was here with me. Something about her tenacity that I had never seen before in a woman. She says she loves me too, but I am not sure if she does. We fuck like beasts, we love hard, and we work our asses off. I will love her forever, but someday I feel she will leave me.

The door opens to our home. She comes into the kitchen where I am drinking my coffee. She sits down in my lap.

"Rough night?" I ask her.

She kisses my cheek.

"Not really, it went smoothly. I was able to get everyone out and call the authority," Tatina says.

"You seriously did not kill any of the vampires?" I ask.

"I killed all of them, but i left the bodies for the authority to deal with," Tatina says.

I kiss the back of her head. She is proud of herself. "Good job," I say to her.

"I was thinking we could spend the day together," Tatina says.

"Sounds good to me," I say.

Spending the day with her, no auctions, no other vampires to deal with, only she and I.

"what do you want to do for the day?" I ask her.

"I was thinking we could spend the day in bed," Tatina says.

I do not think I have touched her in a while. She has been extremely upset recently. Her father passed on, that took a toil on her, then a few bad auctions. I let her bury herself in her work. She always comes back around to me. When she does it is worth the wait.

"Oh really," I say to her.

"Yeah, I know i have been distant, I wanted to take a day to make up for it," Tatina says.

I pull her close to me. "You know I love you. I will go through hell with you," I say to her.

"I know. You are the best thing that has ever happened to me," Tatina says.

"Really, the best thing," I say.

Tatina reaches down and begins rubbing my cock. "Well, you do come with a mighty big bonus," Tatina says.

I lean in to kiss her. Our tongues dance around each other. The amount of electricity and passion between us blows my mind every time we touch. She loves hard and fucks like a champion.

"I am glad you enjoy the perks i offer," I say to her.

I want to carry her to bed, but before I can scoop her up, she is on her knees in front of me. She unzips my pants and pulls out my cock. She is on me devouring me quickly. She slides me in her mouth and down her throat. I rub the back of her head as she pleasures me. I moan with the pleasure she is giving me. She moans as she give me this intense pleasure.

"I want to taste you," I say to her.

She pulls my cock out of her mouth. I help her to her feet. I remove her pants and plant her on the table. I begin eating her pussy in the same place i was having my morning cup of coffee. I slide my tongue in and out of her delicious hot wet pussy. I rub her clit as I enjoy her. She pulls her legs up so I can dive in deeper and deeper.

"Fuck me Draco," She moans.

I lick just a little longer. I love her taste. I cannot get enough of her juices. I want her to cum on my face first. I slide two fingers inside her and suckle her clit. I would love to feed on her thigh while i finger her, but that is a no no. I never feed on her.

"Please fuck me," Tatina begs.

"Cum for me first," I say.

I finger her harder and continue sucking her clit. I can feel her getting tighter and ready to cum for me. I slide a finger into her ass. She begins to cum on my face. I lick all of her juices. I love her taste.

"You better fuck me now!" Tatina demands.

"I am ready now," I say to her.

I stand between her legs ready to insert my cock into her hot wet pussy. I put the tip in just to drive her wild. She puts her legs on my shoulders. I hold onto her legs as i push into her. I thrust deep inside her. Her walls are tightening around my cock.

"Cum for me again," I say.

Tatina moans louder.

I push into her harder and faster. She feels amazing. She is so hot on my cock. I feel her body begin to release again for me. As she cums on my I release my seed into her. I let her legs down. I lean down to kiss her.

"Don't think you are getting off that easy," Tatina says.

"I know, I am yours all day," I say.

I pull out of her. I help her off of our kitchen table. I scoop her up to take her to get a shower. I plan to fuck her all day.

As I carry her up the stairs to our bathroom, she looks up to me and whispers,"I love you more than you will ever know."

That is all I needed. I will care for you for as long as I am alive.

Chapter 37

TATINA POV

Being with Draco these last few years has done something wonderful for me. After surviving the hell Craig put me through, Draco has showed me nothing but love and compassion. I know he loves me, he shows me every single day we are together.

He is patient and kind. He allows me time to decompress and be by myself. It is strange how we became a couple. First he was my rescuer then my best friend, somehow I worked myself into his bed as his lover, but ultimately he became to me the man I needed.

He doesn't feed on me ever. He knows it is something that scares me now. He has never tried but once. I think I almost lost my mind that night. Draco being Draco held me while I cried. He helped me through so much. Then he taught me how to fight for the rights of others. He taught me how to be me. I became a warrior to stop the auctions because of him and him alone.

When I had my worst night rescuing women and men in the auction, he held me all night. He let me cry until the tears stopped. I knew then I loved him. He tells me all the time how important I am to him. He doesn't even know that I feel the same way. I have become hard in the last two years but not where he is concerned. He is my weakness.

I will fight beside him and for him until the end of time. He asked me to marry him more than once. I never said no, but I have not said yes either. I know I will marry him some day. When the pain of yesterday finally stops and I can give myself to him completely I will say yes.

I think because of my special circumstances I am afraid he will want children. I do not want to bring any child into this world that has to worry about an auctioneer stealing them and selling them. I could not live with myself if someone I brought into this world became a hybrid breeder. He has never brought any of it up, but I know he thinks about it. We have a long life ahead of us.

Today is my day with him. I want to lay in the bed snuggled up to his incredible body. I want to hold him and fuck him all day long. I do not want to think about the auction or what it is doing to people. I only want to be his today.

"What are you thinking about?" Draco asks.

"Us," I say as I run my fingers across his stomach.

"I think you are thinking about more than only us," Draco says.

"I was thinking about how much I love you and how I do not think you know it," I say.

"I know you love me," Draco says.

"Do you?" I ask.

"I am the first person you come to when you are happy or sad; that is how I know you love me," Draco says.

"You are the only person in my life, Draco," I say.

"That is not true. You have all these people you have helped. They all adore you," Draco says.

"But not like you. You are everything to me," I say.

I run my fingers down his stomach to his cock. I begin rubbing him. I want him inside me more than ever. I need him today. I do not know why, but today I only want to be here in this bed with him inside me.

"Marry me?" Draco says.

I do not answer. I find it better to ignore him when he asks.

"I wish you would just say no so I would get over it and stop asking you," Draco says.

I continue rubbing his cock. I slide down in the bed to get beneath him. As I am about to slide his cock in my mouth, he stops me.

"Say no, and I will stop asking," Draco says.

"How about I agree to discuss this over dinner?" I ask.

I do not want to ruin the moment. Maybe I will think about it more between now and then.

"I can agree to those terms on one condition," Draco says.

"Hmm, what is that?" I ask him as I slide his cock in and out of my mouth.

"You swing that beautiful ass around and sit on my face," Draco says.

"I can agree to those terms," I say.

I slide his cock in and out of my mouth a few more times, watching him enjoy my mouth. I move to place my pussy right in his face. He begins licking me while I suck his cock. He loves this more than anything, and damn he is good at it. He always takes time to enjoy me and, better yet, making sure everything he does is something I want.

He licks me until I cum on his face. I move my pussy off of his face. I slide my body down to ride him reverse. He holds onto my ass as I lean forward, rocking on his hard cock. His hands run up and down my back. I rock harder thrusting him deep inside me. I slow down as I begin to cum. He is not having it. He pushes up and grinds hard into me, pushing me to orgasm hard. I moan and scream with the ecstasy he is providing me.

I lay my body down, my head at his feet. He begins moving behind me. He pulls my ass up in the air and is positioned behind me while I am still reeling from my last orgasm. He pushed into my pussy. He grips my hips pulling me back to him.

"Cum for me again," Draco moans.

He barrels into me over and over, pushing deeper into me. He leans into me, reaching around to rub my clit as he plows into my pussy.

I begin to cum again. He pulls out of me and moves me onto my back. He divides my legs and dives into my pussy. He thrust into me hard as I cum. As I release my juice onto him, he begins moaning and spilling his seed into me.

He lies beside me. We are both now at the wrong end of the bed. I love when he fucks me like this. He pulls me closer to him.

"Will I get an answer tonight?" Draco asks.

"Yes, I will give you an answer tonight on one condition," I say.

"What is that?" Draco asks.

"You have to cook," I say.

Chapter 38

DRACO POV

I spend the day getting ready for my date with Tatina tonight. I want everything to be perfect for us tonight. No auction business, no other vampires or anything intruding just Tatina and I. I want to cook for her and make love to her. I want more than anything for her to say yes she will marry me. I want her to be my partner forever.

I have purchased all of her favorite things. This would be so much easier if I let the staff prepare our meal, but she wants me to cook for her. I have not cooked for her in a long time.

I did cheat and have my cook make Tatina a cheesecake. I could not do that no matter how hard I try. The steaks and vegetables, I can grill no problem. She can have cheesecake for desert and I will have her.

What is she says no? At least she will finally give me an answer. No matter what she says tonight, I will never stop loving her. She has no idea what she has done for me.

I never thought in a million years I could love someone like her. She brings out something in me that I did not even know existed. I am an old vampire. I have been around a long time. Love has never been something I thought much about. With her, I want to love her for as long as I live.

"How's it coming?" Tatina sneaks up behind me to ask.

I turn around, kiss her softly. "It is torture, we have staff. I could be making love to you while they cook," I say.

"It is special to me when you cook for me," Tatina says.

"Then I have to confess that I did not make the cheesecake," I say.

"Thank goodness, you make a horrible cheesecake," Tatina says.

"Hey! You ate it the last time I made you one," I say.

"No I did not. I threw it out when you left the house and told you I ate it," Tatina says.

It is so good to see her in good spirits. I pull her in close to me. I kiss her forehead. "I love you so much," I say.

"I know you do. I love you too," Tatina says.

"Good then marry me," I say to her.

"No fair, we are supposed to discuss this tonight over dinner," Tatina says.

"I know, but I need an answer," I say.

"You will get one," Tatina says.

Surely she is not toying with me all day just to say no. It would break my heart into a million pieces if she did that to me. I love her more than I ever knew possible. I only want to make her happy.

I continue working on our magical night through the afternoon. She stays hidden. I wonder what she is up to. I put the finishing touches on dinner. I set everything out on the table. I light candles for us. I want to change clothes before my beautiful date comes down to eat with me.

When I get to the bottom of the stairs she is coming down wearing the most beautiful baby blue dress. She hair is down and flowing to her hips. She curled it and pinned a few strands back in braids.

"You look beautiful," I say as she continues down the stairs to me.

I cannot say anything else. I am blown away by the effort she put into our night.

"I need to change," I say.

"No, stay like that, I plan on getting you out of your clothes rather quickly," Tatina says.

"Yes ma'am," I say to her.

I take her hand to walk her to the dining room table. I cannot stop staring at her.

"Stop it, you have seen me dressed up before," Tatina says.

"I have, but tonight it is different," I say.

"Why is that?" Tatina asks.

"Tonight you are doing it all for me," I say.

I pull out her chair, she sits down, and I push her up to the table. I pour her a glass of wine. I fix her plate with everything I know she loves. I set the plate down in front of her.

"Thank you Draco, you are always so kind to me," Tatina says.

"You are most welcome, my lady," I say.

I pour myself a glass of wine and some food. I sit down next to her. She looks amazing tonight.

"I know you hate when I stare at you, but Tatina, you look so beautiful," I say to her.

"Stop it," She says.

"Have you decided?" I ask her.

"Why do you want to marry me? We are happy the way we are, aren't we?" Tatina asks me.

"I am, we are, but I want more," I say to her.

"You know that I do not want to have children," Tatina says.

"I know and that is fine. We have a very hectic lifestyle. I do not think children would fit in. If you ever decide that you did want children, I think we would need to reevaluate how we live," I say.

"I like our life and what we do. I do not think children would fit in to that ever," Tatina says.

"I agree with that completely. Is that what you are worried about? Tatina I have been on this earth a long time. The thought of having children has never crossed my mind. I am happy with us being together. You are all I need," I say.

"Okay that is out of the way," Tatina says.

"Next obstacle?" I ask.

"Why do you love me so much?" Tatina asks.

"I cannot answer that. I have no idea. I love how brave you are. I love you period. I love everything about you. I love you temper. I love your kindness," I say.

"I feel the same way about you. Ever since that first night after we rescued all those women from that horrible auction. You took me in your arms and I knew right then that I loved you. You made love to me for the first time that night," Tatina says.

"Then you cried for hours and I felt like a pig for touching you," I say.

"I am sorry. I told you why. You were so gentle. I never had that before," Tatina says.

I get out of my chair. I kneel in front of her.

"I am going to ask you one last time. No matter what you say I will not ask again. Will you marry me?" I ask her.

Chapter 39

TATINA POV

I look down at my sweet Draco kneeling before me. He has no idea how badly I want to say yes, but I am afraid. The only thing I know to do is be honest with him.

I place my hand on top of his.

"Draco, I want to be perfectly honest with you. I feel that we have always been honest with each other and there is no reason to stop that now," I say to him.

"That is all I want. I want an answer for a change. No matter what you say I will respect that," Draco says.

"There is no doubt in my mind that we love each other. Is that enough?" I ask him.

"Of course, it is enough. I will love you until the end of time," Draco says.

"What is it that you want from me?" I ask him.

"I want you to be my wife. I want you to be my partner in life. I want us to be together forever," Draco says.

"I am your partner and we will always be together. I just don't want to feel owned by someone ever again," I say.

Draco stands from his kneeling position in front of me. He takes his seat back at the table. I know I have upset him.

"Have I ever made you feel owned by me?" Draco asks.

"No, you have not," I answer him.

"Then why in the hell would you say something so horrible to me? Why in the hell would think that low of me, Tatina?" Draco asks.

He is right. At no point in our relationship has he ever made me feel owned by him. Why am I so afraid to let him marry me?

"Tatina, this is breaking me down. I love you. I give you every freedom you could possible want. I am only asking you to be my wife, my partner. I want us to have a bond forever," Draco says.

"Okay," I say.

"Okay, what do you mean okay?" Draco asks.

"I mean then yes, I will marry you," I say.

"Really, you mean it?" Draco asks.

"I do mean it, but maybe we should get married quickly before I change my mind," I say.

"We could drive to Las Vegas and get married tonight," Draco says.

"You seriously want to drive to Las Vegas to get married right now?" I ask him.

"Why not?" Draco asks me.

"Well, there are some places closer if we are willing to let a vampire marry us," I suggest to Draco.

"That is true. I will leave it up to you. We will do whatever you want to do. I am happy you finally said yes," Draco says.

"Wait, I did not say yes. I said okay," I say to him.

"Wait, I have something for you," Draco says.

He leaves to table and runs up the stairs. What on earth is this man doing? He is up the stairs and back down in a flash. He gets back down on his knee and presents me with a small ring box.

"Tatina Maria, Will you be my partner in life forever?" Draco asks me again while opening the small box for me to see what is inside.

"Yes," I say.

He takes the princess cut diamond out of the box and slips it onto my ring finger.

"If you are serious about doing this tonight, I am more than ready," Draco says.

"Let's do it," I say.

"Okay, Las Vegas or New Orleans?" Draco asks.

"I never want to go back to New Orleans," I say to him.

"I know there is a priest right outside of the city that could marry us tonight and it is a short drive. I promise not to take you into the city for any reason," Draco says.

"Call the priest, if he can do it tonight I am willing to go, if not we can drive to Las Vegas. It would be a nice road trip and we could stop in a hotel along the way," I say to him.

I really do not want to go anywhere near New Orleans. A long drive to Las Vegas would be wonderful, but I know Draco wants to do this right away. He is terrified if given too much time I will change my mind. To be honest I might. My love for him or his love my me is not the issue. I know it is my fear of ever being captive again.

I do not know what I had planned for tonight. I wanted it to be special. I wanted him to feel love and then maybe I was going to let him down easy. Instead I agreed to be his life partner. In reality I already am in partner. He has taken care of me for so long, maybe I should give him this special moment. I will grow into the idea of being his wife.

Draco comes back with a long face. "Father Malone is unable to marry us tonight but there is another priest willing to do it," Draco says.

"Well that is fine. There other priest will be okay," I say to him.

"Yeah, about that, the other priest is in the city," Draco says.

"Oh, I see," I say.

"We don't have to do it, but I have to let him know now," Draco says.

"As long as you are with me I will be okay," I say.

"I am going to call him now. I will offer to pay him to meet us outside of the city," Draco says.

"That is fine. I don't want to go back there ever," I say to him.

"I know. I will see what kind of arrangements I can make," Draco says.

"I can book us a hotel in Westwego. See if he can come there," I say.

"You got it love," Draco says.

Draco rushes off to make the arrangements with the new priest. If I have to go into the city I will, but I do not want to go if it can be avoided.

Chapter 40

DRACO POV

I cannot believe she finally said yes to me. I have waited so long for this moment for us. I hate that the only priest I can find is in the city. I hope if I offer him enough money he will come to a hotel outside of the city and marry us there, if not I will protect her.

There isn't a threat to her anymore. Craig is dead. I made sure of that myself. He cannot come after her. She still fears him. I understand these feelings she has of fear. I cannot say that I would not be the same way if I was in her shoes.

Tatina has developed into the strongest person I have ever known. She walks into auction houses and slave houses. She destroys the idiots that hurt women. She is fearless except for the one fear she is still trying to get passed.

I pack us a small bag for the night. I let her relax while I grab us a few things. We can eat when we get there. She doesn't really want to eat my horrible cooking, it was a test to see if I would do as she asked. She can say what she wants but I know she was only trying to see how serious I was about tonight.

I text the staff to let them know there is a lot of food here, if it's edible eat it, if not throw it out. I grab the wedding rings I purchased for us out of my night stand drawer and the overnight bag and head to her.

She is still sitting at the table. "You know you look like a bride tonight," I say to her.

"I will need clothes for tomorrow," Tatina says.

I pat the bag hanging from my shoulder. "I handled everything," I say to her.

"What about wedding rings," She asks.

"I handled that also," I say.

"What about all of this food?" Tatina asks.

"Well, I text the staff, everything is handled if you want to quit stalling," I say.

"I haven't called the hotel yet," Tatina says.

"You can do that in the car," I say.

"I guess it is settled then, we are getting married," Tatina says.

"Not if you don't want to marry me," I say.

"Yes, I do. Now let's do this," Tatina says.

She gets up from the table. She grabs a bottle of wine from the table. "For the road," Tatina says.

"I want you sober when you say I do," I say to her.

"I will be, but it is for my nerves," Tatina says.

"Okay, but you cannot drink the entire bottle. After we are married we will get a bottle of champagne to celebrate," I say to her.

"After we are married you are going to make love to me as my husband before we do anything else," Tatina says.

"I can live with those conditions," I say to her.

I open the front door for her. She walks out of the house to the car and waits for me to open the door.

"My beautiful lady," I say as I open the car door.

I throw the bag in the trunk and get into the car.

I start the car. "You know you have made me happier than I ever thought possible," I say to her.

"You have me as well," Tatina says.

We drive to the outskirts of New Orleans. I am careful not to get to close to the city. I do not want her to even have to look at it.

I pull into the hotel. We give the car to the valet and head to check in to our room.

"Is he going to come here?" Tatina asks.

"Yes, money always talks my dear," I say to her.

This is not entirely true, I reminded Father Malone how Tatina had saved his niece after that he cancelled his plans and made arrangements to come to the hotel himself.

"Are you up to something?" Tatina asks me.

"No I was only thinking about how I cannot wait to be inside you," I say to her.

"Pervert," she says as she smacks me on the ass.

"Who is the pervert now," I say to her.

When we get to the room, I call Father Malone to let him know what room we are in at the hotel.

"He will be here in twenty minutes," I tell Tatina.

"Good, let's make this quick. I have plans for you tonight," Tatina says.

"You do, why don't you tell me about it while we wait on the priest," I say to her.

"No sir, I am a lady. What I want to do to you is very unlady like," Tatina says.

She is feeling playful tonight and I love it. I pull her into my arms and hold her. I kiss her forehead.

"I love you," I say to her.

"I love you too," Tatina says.

"We can take some time off to just be together if you want for a little while," I say to her. I stroke her hair and rub her back. She needs time off.

"We cannot do that for long. Maybe a few days, but you know there are people who need us," Tatina says.

"What about you? You never think about yourself." I say to her.

"I am fine, Draco. I need to work. It keeps my mind occupied," Tatina says.

"I promise if we take a few weeks off that I will keep you very occupied," I say to her.

"Well, then, I may have to take you up on that offer," Tatina says.

There is a knock on the door interrupting our moment.

"Last chance to back out," I say.

"Never, you are stuck with me now," Tatina says.

"I am serious. If you want to change your mind do it now. I will not be angry. We can make love all night and get up in the morning and go back to the way we were. I would be upset but I only want you to do this if you are sure," I say to her.

"I am positive. I wasn't sure earlier but I am now," Tatina say.

She goes to open the door to let the priest in to our room. In only a few moments she will be my wife and finally we can live out our lives and be happy as she deserves.

This story continues in Weekend in New Orleans coming in 2022

Also by Lillith Mykals Kennedy

The Alpha's Caged Pet
The Alpha's Caged Pet

The Vampire Authority
I Belong to a Wolf
The Auction

Standalone
Dirty Little Secret
Flames In The Fire
Her Obsession
The Alpha's Fairy
The Auction Series